As a child she had been devoted to him,

wanting only to be with him.

To her horror, now she found she wanted more. As a woman she wanted him to regard her with smoldering intensity, then to deliver on the look by taking her in his arms. Her whole body vibrated at the very thought, and she shivered.

"Is something wrong, Eleanor?"

His use of the name punctured the fantasy. "You're right. I'm a little tired after the flight."

She was glad of the excuse to be shown straight to her suite as soon as they entered the palace, feeling that she needed the time alone to regroup. The first thing she had to do was call Eleanor and tell her that this wasn't going to work. How could Caroline convince Michel that, as Eleanor, she couldn't marry him, when it was the very thing Caroline wanted for herself?

THE CARRAMER CROWN

Dear Reader,

Though August is already upon us, we've got yet another month of special 20th anniversary titles sure to prolong your summer reading pleasure.

STORKVILLE, USA, our newest in-line continuity, launches this month with Marie Ferrarella's *Those Matchmaking Babies*. In this four-book series, the discovery of twin babies abandoned on a day care center's doorstep leads to secrets being revealed...and unsuspecting townsfolk falling in love!

Judy Christenberry rounds up THE CIRCLE K SISTERS with *Cherish the Boss*, in which an old-school cowboy and a modern woman find themselves at odds—and irresistibly attracted to each other! In Cara Colter's memorable VIRGIN BRIDES offering, the "world's oldest living virgin" meets the man she hopes will be her *First Time, Forever.*

Valerie Parv's THE CARRAMER CROWN continues, as a woman long in love with Michel de Marigny poses as *The Prince's Bride-To-Be*. Arlene James delights with *In Want of a Wife*, the story of a self-made millionaire who is looking for a mother for his adopted daughter—and, could it be, a wife for himself? And Natalie Patrick offers the charming *His, Hers...Ours?*, in which a marriage-wary pair play parents and discover they like it—and each other—far too much.

Next month, look for another installment of STORKVILLE, USA, and the launch of THE CHANDLERS REQUEST...from *New York Times* bestselling author Kasey Michaels.

Happy Reading!

Mary-Theresa Hussey

Mary-Theresa Hussey
Senior Editor

Please address questions and book requests to:
Silhouette Reader Service
U.S.: 3010 Walden Ave., P.O. Box 1325, Buffalo, NY 14269
Canadian: P.O. Box 609, Fort Erie, Ont. L2A 5X3

The Prince's
Bride-To-Be

VALERIE PARV

Silhouette

ROMANCE™

Published by Silhouette Books

America's Publisher of Contemporary Romance

To my manager and friend, Linda Tate, with thanks

 SILHOUETTE BOOKS

ISBN 0-373-19465-X

THE PRINCE'S BRIDE-TO-BE

Copyright © 2000 by Valerie Parv

Visit Silhouette at www.eHarlequin.com

Printed in U.S.A.

Books by Valerie Parv

Silhouette Romance

The Leopard Tree #507
The Billionaire's Baby Chase #1270
Baby Wishes and Bachelor Kisses #1313
*The Monarch's Son #1459
*The Prince's Bride-To-Be #1465

*The Carramer Crown

VALERIE PARV

lives and breathes romance, and has even written a guide to being romantic, crediting her cartoonist husband of nearly thirty years as her inspiration. As a former buffalo and crocodile hunter in Australia's Northern Territory, he's ready-made hero material, she says.

When not writing her novels and nonfiction books, or speaking about romance on Australian radio and television, Valerie enjoys dollhouses, being a *Star Trek* fan and playing with food (in cooking that is). Valerie agrees with actor Nichelle Nichols, who said, "The difference between fantasy and fact is that fantasy simply hasn't happened yet."

HISTORY OF CARRAMER

The Carramer Crown takes place in the fictitious island kingdom of Carramer in the South Pacific. French explorer la Perouse called Carramer "the loveliest fleet of islands anchored in any ocean." Carramer comprises three inhabited islands and a handful of tiny offshore islands. The main island is Celeste, home to the capital city of Solano, and the ruling monarch, Lorne de Marigny. Across the Carramer Strait lies the larger, blissfully beautiful Isle des Anges (Island of the Angels) and its near neighbor, tiny Nuee, both governed by Prince Lorne's younger brother, Michel, next in line to the throne after Lorne's son, Nori. Younger sister Adrienne sees no role for herself in government and yearns to establish a horsebreeding stable.

Carramer's traditions are a mixture of French and Polynesian influences. It enjoys a perfect climate, as near-constant trade winds prevail throughout the year, and most rain falls as daytime showers that are accompanied by rainbows, giving rise to the popular name for Carramer, "the Rainbow Isles."

There is rumored to be another royal offspring living in the United States, but so far that story remains untold.

Valerie Parv
Official historian to the sovereign state of Carramer

Prologue

His Royal Highness Prince Michel de Marigny couldn't take his gaze off the magazine his brother, Prince Lorne, had left for him. On the cover a model posed against the distinctive Manhattan skyline, half a world away from the island kingdom of Carramer.

The model, Eleanor Temple, had hair the color and style of a lion's mane and an intriguing heart-shaped face. Her eyes reminded Michel of a cat's. They were an unusual amber color, and even the flatness of the photograph couldn't conceal the challenge sparkling out of them from under a fringe of golden lashes.

Aware of his boss's preoccupation, the prince's assistant moved around the office quietly attending to his duties. I should be doing the same, Michel thought. As governor of the island provinces Isle des Anges and Nuee, he had more than enough demands on his time. But he remained transfixed by the photograph.

Pausing at the prince's desk, the assistant placed a stack

of documents awaiting signature into the in-tray. "She's beautiful, Your Highness. Who is she?"

Michel looked up. "My bride-to-be."

The man's body language telegraphed his shock. Michel could almost hear him wondering how the country's playboy prince, regularly named as one of the world's most eligible bachelors, could have a bride-to-be, far less one who was an American cover model.

"Sir?"

Michel sighed. "It's quite a story, Andre. I'll tell you about it sometime."

His assistant left and Michel reached for the documents, but his hand stilled as he recalled a sunlit day fifteen years before. Living on Carramer's main island of Celeste as guests of the de Marigny royal family were American anthropologist Dr. August Temple and his identical twin daughters, Eleanor and Caroline. In his two years in Carramer, Dr. Temple had become fascinated by the ancient ceremonies, especially one in which the eldest female child of a clan was promised in marriage to a son of the royal family.

The monarch had been a keen amateur historian, and had commissioned Dr. Temple to study the history of the Mayat people, so Michel wasn't surprised when his father had agreed to Dr. Temple's request to stage a reenactment of the betrothal ceremony between his daughter and one of the princes. What had caught Michel unawares was being chosen to participate.

"Shouldn't Lorne do it? He's the eldest. I'm only thirteen," he had said, when his father explained what the anthropologist wanted him to do.

"Lorne is preparing for important exams. His studies take precedence," his father had replied. "Besides, I thought you liked Eleanor Temple."

Michel turned up his nose. "I like Caroline better. She's good fun and she likes the same things I do, but I don't want to marry her either. They're girls."

His father had looked amused. "It is usual to take a girl as one's wife." Then he had grown stern. "It is decided. The ceremony will go ahead."

When his father used what Michel called his "royal" tone, he knew better than to argue. He had been unable to resist a parting question over his shoulder, "It is only pretense, isn't it, sir? I won't really be married to Eleanor, will I?"

His father's eyes had twinkled. "Of course you won't be married to her. A betrothal isn't the same as a wedding." He hadn't added that a betrothal was, however, a promise to marry. And Michel had been too young and in awe of his father to think of asking any more questions.

He had spent the next few days with his tutor, learning the Old Carramer words of the ceremony. When the time came, he was dressed in what he privately thought was a stupid costume of tight pants and a leather vest, with a traditional Mayat feathered cloak around his shoulders.

When he stepped out into the fresh air where a canopy had been set up overlooking the ocean, he felt acutely self-conscious. He wasn't reassured by the sight of eleven-year-old Eleanor waiting for him, wearing a flowing white gown with a garland of wildflowers in her hair. Despite his father's assurance, she looked too much like a bride for his liking. Until she caught sight of him and made a face, earning a reprimand from her father.

Michel glanced at Eleanor's twin sister, Caroline, who was watching from the sidelines. He noticed that she looked as unhappy as he felt, as if she would rather be anywhere else but here. She and Eleanor looked so much alike that he couldn't explain why he felt more drawn to Caroline. He only knew that he did. She enjoyed talking about his hobby of studying dolphins, and she loved coming with him to look for shells on the beach. Unlike Eleanor, Caroline never complained about getting sand in her shoes.

Michel understood why Eleanor had been chosen for the ceremony. She was the oldest, even if it was only by a few minutes. But Caroline would have made it so much more fun, and they could have laughed about it afterward during one of their long heart-to-heart talks. Eleanor looked so serious that Michel wanted to remind her that it was only a reenactment. It wasn't real.

Like his father and Dr. Temple, Eleanor acted as if it was the most solemn occasion in the world. It would be many years later before Michel found out that it had been.

Michel forced his mind back to the present and his conversation with Lorne that morning. The brothers had known for a long time that the betrothal ceremony was binding, and Michel suspected that his father had known it, too, letting it go ahead in the hope of taming his headstrong younger son.

Faint hope, Michel thought. His reputation as the playboy prince wasn't entirely undeserved, although the media made more of it than was warranted by his actions. And as Lorne had pointed out this morning, adopting a baby boy who was rumored to be Michel's love child wasn't the most discreet action he could have taken, but he was too devoted to baby Luc now to let public opinion come between them. And he had never allowed his life-style to interfere with his royal duties.

Even Lorne had been forced to agree. "I didn't say you had. But, since you've taken on the responsibility of a child, he should have a stable family environment. I'm not urging you to marry for the sake of it," he had said as he paced Michel's office. "My own experience taught me what hell marriage can be when it's to the wrong person. But before Chandra died, she gave me a wonderful son, so how can I say it was a mistake? Now I have Allie and the baby, and I want you to know the same happiness they have brought me."

Michel mustered a smile. This wasn't coming from the ruler of Carramer but from the concerned older brother. "Where do you find another like Allie?"

"Maybe you already have." And Lorne had dropped the magazine on Michel's desk, indicating the American beauty on the cover. "You are legally betrothed to her, after all."

"None of us understood what we were doing at the time," Michel defended himself.

"It doesn't make the ceremony any less binding."

"There must be a way to break the contract."

"Instead of spending time on that, why not send for Eleanor and remind her of your obligation to each other?"

Michel frowned. "Eleanor is unlikely to agree to marry me because of a ceremony we went through when we were children."

"Then make her want to marry you," Lorne said in the unmistakable tone of a royal decree. His expression eased slightly. "Judging from her present appearance, conquering Eleanor Temple should present an interesting challenge."

Michel smiled wryly in recognition of being known too well. "I never could resist a challenge." In a strange way, he thought he might even enjoy it.

Chapter One

The limousine waiting on the tarmac at Aviso Airport flew the blue-and-jade standard of the Carramer Royal House. Flanked by motorcycle police, it was an impressive sight and a reminder to Caroline Temple that there was no turning back now. Her stomach fluttered ominously at what she was about to do.

She would never be able to convince Prince Michel that she was Eleanor, she thought in sudden panic. After Eleanor had received the prince's summons and realized that he really expected her to come to Carramer and marry him because of a betrothal contract made when they were children, Eleanor had begged her to change places. Now, Caroline wasn't so sure she could carry it off.

With Eleanor about to become engaged to the man she loved, heir to a Californian fortune, she could hardly come herself. Her intended's mother already disapproved of Eleanor's modeling career. Discovering that her prospective daughter-in-law was already engaged to someone else would be the last straw.

It was all their father's fault, Caroline thought in frustration. This time the eccentric anthropologist had gone too far. What they had all thought was harmless playacting had turned out to be a real betrothal ceremony based on ancient Carramer tradition. As a result, Caroline's twin sister was now legally promised to the heir to the Carramer throne whom they'd last seen when he was thirteen and the twins were eleven years old.

"I guess I'm not in Kansas anymore," Caroline murmured to herself, unconsciously straightening her back as she was escorted across the tarmac toward the cavalcade. In truth she was as far from Kansas as one could get, on Carramer's second largest island, Isle des Anges, governed by His Royal Highness Prince Michel de Marigny.

From the air, she had easily picked out the distinctive shape, like an angel's wings, that gave the island its name. Across the Carramer Strait she had spotted the main island, Celeste, where the twins and their father had lived for almost two years, in the capital city of Solano. The only island she had yet to set foot on was Nuee, located at the tip of Isle des Anges like the dot on an exclamation point, and her searching gaze had located it easily as they came in to land.

Alerted by some invisible process, an official had helped her from the plane ahead of the other passengers, giving Eleanor's passport no more than a cursory glance. Not that a closer look would have raised any eyebrows. Caroline knew she looked the spitting image of her twin. How she felt was another matter.

Eleanor had put her modeling skills to good use, showing Caroline how to highlight her amber eyes with a clear mascara that made her lashes look incredibly long and silky. Her shoulder-length hair had been curled and fluffed out in imitation of Eleanor's trademark lion's mane. More used to wearing it tied back, Caroline kept wanting to brush the strands off her face.

Her casual clothes had given way to a tailored pantsuit in aubergine linen, dressed with a cream-and-gold Hermès scarf and gold hoops weighing down her ears. Her leather suitcases were filled with Eleanor's clothes, although she had protested at including her twin's gold bikini instead of her own more modest maillot.

"Michel won't have a clue what you usually wear when you swim," she protested when Eleanor argued. The thought of the prince seeing her in something as revealing as the bikini disturbed Caroline for some reason.

"We're talking image here," Eleanor had said, defiantly putting the bikini back in the case, obviously determined not to let Caroline win the argument. "To be convincing you have to live as me twenty-four hours a day."

"That explains the lace negligees," Caroline had commented wryly. Eleanor had pounced on the T-shirts Caroline usually wore to bed, throwing them aside in favor of the more glamorous nightwear Eleanor herself favored. Caroline consoled herself with the thought that she wouldn't have to wear the sexy garments in front of Michel, but it didn't stop her from blushing at the sight of them in the suitcase.

"When did we stop dressing alike?" she asked Eleanor. It seemed they had never made the decision consciously but had gravitated toward their individual styles sometime during their teens.

"When I discovered rich men," her twin had responded, not entirely in jest. As a teenager she had vowed to marry well to avoid the insecure life they had known with their father. In Danny O'Hare-Smith, she had found the man of her dreams.

Ironically, it seemed to Caroline now, she had declared

she preferred to be a princess, little guessing that she would be called upon to act the part as an adult.

Eleanor didn't want any part of royal life, Caroline knew. In her sister's eyes, a title involved too much duty and obligation. However rich the de Marignys might be, spending their money would be a problem. Royals perceived as being too free-spending invariably attracted criticism, Eleanor had pointed out.

Danny, on the other hand, offered Eleanor a life of ease and comfort without as much accountability and with the added bonus of his adoration thrown in. All Eleanor had to do was what she did best, look glamorous and adore Danny in return.

Caroline knew it wouldn't be enough to satisfy her. It must be her father's influence driving her to make her own way in the world. He had used his inherited wealth to explore other cultures and record their traditions for posterity. While not sharing his obsession with the past, she had inherited his willingness to work for what she wanted. Everything worth having came with a price.

The price of Caroline's own deception was only too evident the moment she reached the limousine. A uniformed driver opened the rear door and Prince Michel uncoiled from the back seat, offering her his hand in greeting. "Welcome back to Carramer, Eleanor."

As he straightened and her fingers brushed his outstretched hand, a sense of shock rippled through her. The photograph he had sent with the summons hadn't exaggerated. If anything it had understated Michel's masculine appeal. The boy she had once played with in the palace grounds at Solano was a distant echo from the man in front of her. A devilish glint lit his pewter gaze and a shock of hair strayed across a high forehead. Over the years his hair had darkened to the color of burned toast and a faint dusting of premature gray at the temples made him look wonderfully distinguished.

These days his six-foot-one height was housed in a well-built frame that his impeccably tailored pants and white sports shirt did little to disguise. The expensive fabric strained across his broad shoulders and tucked in at a narrow waist. A crocodile-leather belt cinched in his pants above lean hips and long legs.

She felt her cheeks heat as she forced her gaze back to his face. The classical features of his de Marigny heritage were still evident, but the set of his strong jaw was all his own, speaking of a stubbornness she remembered only too well. From the look of him it had only intensified in the man.

Sucking in a sharp breath, she refused to let herself step back. "Hello, Michel. It's been a long time."

"Much too long." The prince rested both hands lightly on her shoulders and bent to kiss her cheek. It was hardly a kiss in the romantic sense, but at the touch of his lips, a dizziness assailed her that had little to do with the heat of the day. It took a lot to keep her hands decorously at her sides.

When he lifted his head, he looked startled, as if the kiss had affected him, too. Did he suspect she was a fraud, she wondered in alarm, then dismissed the worry. He was probably just stunned that the girl he remembered was a woman now. Her own difficulty in accepting the man in the boy she had once known suggested as much. How else could she explain the way her internal temperature soared and her pulse quickened at his fleeting touch?

"It's good to see you again," he said, his voice deep and thrilling.

Goose bumps peppered her spine. He meant it was good to see Eleanor, Caroline reminded herself as a pang seized her, its intensity catching her unawares. She had known this wouldn't be easy, but she hadn't counted on feeling such a strong resurgence of her childhood crush on Michel. She should be pleased that he had accepted her as her twin without demur, but it bothered her for some reason.

In the short time available to them since they received Michel's summons, Eleanor had schooled Caroline in how to walk, talk and behave like her twin, but underneath she still felt like Caroline Temple and part of her wanted the prince's welcome to be for her. In your dreams, she told herself sternly, knowing that was where such fantasies belonged.

It didn't help that she felt like someone caught in a dream as Michel helped her into the luxurious car. If she wasn't careful, it would be very easy to confuse fantasy and reality.

When they were comfortably settled, the limousine smoothly pulled onto the freeway out of the airport, the escort clearing the way for them. She was thankful that the roominess of the vehicle allowed her to put some much-needed space between them. It wasn't only Michel's impressive physique that threatened to overwhelm her. He had an air of mastery that made her feel fragile and protected, not a feeling she was used to. For most of their lives, she and Eleanor had more or less parented themselves while August Temple was busy with his anthropological quests. Michel's capable, caring aura was a novelty.

Was that why she had felt more comfortable around unreliable men like Ralph Devonport? she asked herself. She had believed herself in love with him until he betrayed her with another woman the moment her back was turned. She had known he had a roving eye but had believed him when he told her he was merely counting his blessings. It had taken her a while to work out how many "blessings" Ralph had felt he needed. After him, a man who had waited almost fifteen years for a woman struck Caroline as a prince in more ways than one.

With Michel beside her, it was difficult to recall what Ralph looked like, Caroline thought in consternation. Ralph had caused her so much heartache, but after a few minutes in the prince's company she was having trouble thinking of any man but him. What was going on here?

"Did you enjoy your flight?" Michel asked, startling her back to reality.

"For my first experience of flying first class, it was great," she responded without thinking, still troubled by his effect on her.

"I would have thought you'd be used to it in your line of work."

Just in time she remembered she was supposed to be a jet-setting model. "I'm not quite in the supermodel league yet," she said with a light laugh, trying to recall whether Eleanor had ever flown first class. She didn't think so.

"If your photo on the cover of *World Style* magazine is a guide, it won't be long," he said graciously.

Eleanor would have accepted the compliment as her due, so Caroline masked her discomfort and nodded. "I see you've been keeping tabs."

He drew an almost imperceptible breath before asking, "Are you surprised?"

She had been wondering how to bring up the subject. "Because we're supposed to be engaged, you mean? Michel, we need to talk about that."

His hawklike profile faced her, so she couldn't see his eyes, but his mouth tightened slightly. "I'd prefer us to get reacquainted before we discuss our betrothal."

Her hopes of resolving this quickly and being on her way to America were instantly dashed, but part of her exulted in his decision. She resisted the feeling. The longer she stayed, the more chance she had of being unmasked as an impostor. It didn't stop her spirits from lifting at the prospect of spending more time with him.

"How is your twin sister?" he asked.

Caroline gathered her wits. "She's fine. She runs a floral design business called Temple of Green, designing themes for weddings and society events."

He nodded as if the information wasn't news to him. "I gather she is also successful in her work."

"She loves what she does, and her clients say it shows."

"Caroline always did love flowers."

Telling herself she was imagining the faintly wistful note in his voice, Caroline glanced at him curiously. "Yes, she did, didn't she. Remember when we were children, she would pick flowers from the palace gardens to make bouquets and garlands?"

He nodded. "Barefoot and decked with flowers, she used to remind me of a wood nymph. Her choice of career should suit her perfectly."

Caroline had no trouble being honest. "Most of the time it does."

He slanted his body toward her. "Only most of the time?"

The sharpness in his voice told her she had piqued his interest. There was no choice but to go on. "She hasn't been all that lucky in love. Not long ago a man let her down badly."

"In what way?"

"She found him with another woman," she admitted, waiting for the familiar fist of pain to close around her heart. It did, but far less strongly than she expected. She hated to think she was so shallow that she was getting over Ralph already, until a glance at the man beside her made her wonder again if he had something to do with it.

His dark eyebrows arced downward. "Poor Caroline. Was she badly hurt?"

"Yes, but I—I told her he wasn't worth breaking her heart over." Caroline heard her voice falter but felt it was dangerous to encourage this line of discussion. Michel probably only asked after her out of courtesy, not because he really wanted to know the details.

She depressed the window control and the glass slid down to admit the fragrant Carramer air as the car purred along. She was gratified to recognize where she was. They would soon be at Michel's palace at Turtle Bay on the outskirts of Aviso. Caroline was glad that letters from Michel's sister, Adrienne, had kept her up to date with such details.

Memories of the carefree times they had spent on this island as children assailed her along with the scent of ginger and wild orchids. As a boy, Michel and his family had lived at the royal palace at Solano, on the main island of Celeste, but Isle des Anges—the aptly named island of angels—had been a favorite recreational retreat for the royal family. She was pleased to see that time hadn't distorted her memory of its beauty. She inhaled deeply. "I never dreamed that the next time I came to Anges you would be governor of the whole province."

"And of Nuee. I administer both islands," he explained, sounding faintly amused. "What did you expect me to end up doing?"

Recalling his boyhood passions, she felt a smile bloom. "Probably diving on some coral reef looking for new species of sea creatures or trying to communicate with spotted dolphins."

He laughed and the mellow sound rolled over her like a caress. "I still do all those things, but marine biology is strictly a hobby these days. As my brother, Lorne, is fond of reminding me, as a member of the royal house of Carramer, I have responsibilities.''

She doubted whether Michel needed any reminding. As a boy he had taken his position seriously, although he had never been pompous about it. ''It's still hard to think of you as an heir to the throne,'' she confessed. ''Did I put my foot in it by addressing you as Michel instead of Your Royal Highness?''

He shook his head. ''You never stood on ceremony when we were children. I don't expect you to start now. In any case, titles are hardly appropriate between us, under the circumstances.''

Like a shower of cold water, his reminder awoke Caroline to reality. No matter how attractive he was, he was effectively off-limits as long as he was betrothed to Eleanor. Even if Caroline succeeded in her mission to extricate her twin from the commitment, it wouldn't help her own cause. The deception would ensure he never wanted anything to do with either of them again.

''How are Lorne and Adrienne?'' she asked to distract herself.

''My brother is the best ruler Carramer has ever had,'' Michel admitted easily. ''He's deeply in love with his Australian wife, Allie, who gave him a baby daughter, Aimee, not long ago, a sister to Crown Prince Nori, who is six.''

She couldn't suppress a stab of envy. Lorne had always been the distant one, too preoccupied with his duties as heir to the throne to have much to do with the twins. He was the last person Caroline had expected to hear had fallen madly in love. ''I'm happy for him,'' she said sincerely. ''And your sister?''

Michel's taut expression eased, and she remembered how fond he was of his younger sibling. ''Adrienne is in Paris at the moment, attending some international conference on horse breeding. I gather she and Caroline still exchange letters,'' he added.

Caroline felt her face fall. "What a shame she's away. I was looking forward to seeing her again.''

He regarded her curiously. "Surely you will? She's taking a holiday in Provence after the conference, but she'll be home in a couple of months.''

It was longer than Caroline hoped to have to remain in Carramer, pretending to be Eleanor, but she could hardly say so when Michel clearly thought she was here to stay. "I mean I was looking forward to seeing her sooner,'' she amended. "I suppose she still lives in the capital?''

"Yes, but not at the royal palace. Now that Lorne is happily married, she says the country doesn't need another first lady so she set up her own home in Solano. Although, as Lorne likes to remind me, they see much more of Adrienne than me at the palace.''

"I suppose you have too much to do governing Isle des Anges and Nuee,'' Caroline observed.

"It's as good a reason as any to stay away,'' he told her with an odd note in his voice.

Something turned over inside Caroline. Michel had always been the fun-loving brother of the pair, the playboy prince, as the international gossip columns called him. She shouldn't be surprised if he found his brother's cozy domesticity trying, but it bothered her for some reason. Something in his tone suggested that it wasn't the whole story.

"Tell me about Eleanor Temple,'' he urged.

For a horrific moment she thought he had guessed her true identity, and felt herself pale until she realized his use of the third person was a royal habit, nothing more. "What would you like to know?''

"The usual things. Where you went after you left Carramer, what you did. How your sister ended up working with flowers and you got started in modeling. Adrienne shared Caroline's letters with me so I know some details but not as much as I'd like to know."

His reply defused her fear that he had somehow guessed the truth. He only wanted to fill in the gap created by the years. He still didn't know that the letter writer was riding in the limousine with him. It made her less likely to betray herself, but the thought gave her no joy. She didn't like lying to him. It was as simple as that.

She decided to stick to the facts as much as possible. "After we left here, we went to the Northern Territory of Australia, to Arnhem Land, where Dad studied aboriginal culture and rock art. I thought it would be tropical, like Carramer, but it was monsoonal for half the year and arid the other half. The red dust got into everything. We used to joke that we'd turn into redheads because of the dust."

"Instead, you turned into beautiful women," he commented. From a seat pocket he pulled out a copy of *World Style* magazine. It was bent back at the article about Eleanor, Caroline noticed. A corner had been turned down next to a photograph of the twins together, taken outside their grandmother's house in California.

She explained about inheriting the house. "I use it as the base for my modeling career and Caroline runs her floral design business from it."

"You still look alike although Caroline wears her hair differently," he commented, glancing from the picture back to her.

If she had really been Eleanor, she would have been irritated by his continual references to her twin, she thought. Instead she found it confusing. "Caroline always preferred simple things," she said.

He brushed a forefinger over the picture and she felt a

shiver slide down her spine. "I'd call her style natural rather than simple."

"Caroline would probably agree," she said with total honesty. Spending so much of her childhood close to nature in subsistence villages, she had learned to value people far more than material possessions. She turned away so he wouldn't see how much his comment had touched her. The feeling of being understood was heartening but much too dangerous. It was Eleanor he needed to understand, not Caroline.

She found her voice with an effort. "After Australia we lived in Vila in Vanuatu for a while, then in a village along the Sepik River in Papua New Guinea, until Dad took us back to the States to complete our education. Afterward, we decided to settle there."

"It sounds as if your life-style provided quite an education already."

She nodded. "Dad made sure we kept up our studies by correspondence no matter where we lived, but—" She left the sentence unfinished.

"You would have preferred a settled home and a more conventional life," he guessed with uncanny accuracy.

She knew her expression confirmed it. "I used to envy children who were born and grew up in the same place. They knew who they were, where they belonged."

"Now you belong here," he said with a certainty that touched her heart. For a moment, she wished... She dismissed the half-formed desire. If anyone belonged here, it was Eleanor and she wanted no part of it. What Caroline wanted didn't enter into it.

"Michel, we must talk about that," Caroline said on a note of desperation.

"In time. We have arrived at the palace."

As he spoke the limousine and its escort glided to a halt

outside a building she recognized from the photo Michel had sent to Eleanor. They stopped beneath a soaring porte cochere supported by columns sculpted from Italian marble that blended flawlessly with the coral-colored local stone structure of the palace itself. It was surrounded by dozens of brilliantly colored bougainvilleas, citrus and palm trees, flower gardens, lagoons, fountains and waterfalls.

Caroline was surprised at how quickly the memories rushed back. Looking around, she glimpsed the sunken tennis court on which she and the royal children had played fiercely competitive matches. Beyond it was a landscaped walkway leading down the cliff side to a marina, where a fleet of pleasure craft were probably still moored. Michel's parents had often included the twins in their family expeditions to Isles des Anges.

"I was sorry to hear about your parents," she said, turning to Michel.

"We appreciated your father's call and the flowers you sent," the prince said, emotion burring his voice.

She touched Michel's hand, sharing his sense of loss. His parents had made her feel welcome. She had been devastated when Adrienne wrote to her about their deaths in a cyclone that had swept the main island twelve years ago, sharing in her royal friend's grief. Bereft of relatives of their own within close proximity, the twins had become attached to Michel's family while they lived in Carramer. "Your father used to call us his little princesses," she said nostalgically.

"He thought Lorne and I should each marry one of you," Michel told her.

She regarded him in surprise. "Did he now? Who did he have in mind for Lorne?"

"You, of course, as the elder by a couple of minutes,"

he said, his eyes dancing. "He felt it was right for the younger brother to marry the younger sister."

Since it had been Caroline's own fantasy when she was a child, she could hardly argue. "What did you think?" she couldn't help asking.

"I think fate has a way of working these things out," he said diplomatically. "In any event, Lorne was away studying when your father arranged the betrothal ceremony, so the question never arose. We'd better go inside. You must be tired after your journey."

As an answer, it was no answer. And it left Caroline no wiser as to whom Michel would have chosen if things had been different. He was right, they weren't different, she told herself irritably. Sitting beside him in the limousine, she was aware of her old crush gripping her with almost suffocating force. As a child she had been devoted to him, wanting only to be with him and have him look at her with affection.

To her horror she found it was still what she wanted, but now she wanted more. As a woman she wanted him to regard her with smoldering intensity, then to deliver on the look by taking her in his arms. Her whole body vibrated like a tuning fork at the very thought, and she shivered.

He glanced at her in concern. "Is something wrong, Eleanor?"

His use of the name punctured the fantasy. "Everything's fine. You're right, I'm a little tired after the flight."

She was glad of the excuse to be shown straight to her suite as soon as they entered the palace, feeling that she needed the time alone to regroup. The first thing she had to do was call Eleanor and tell her that this wasn't going to work. How could Caroline convince Michel that, as Eleanor, she couldn't marry him when it was the very thing Caroline was starting to fear she wanted for herself?

Chapter Two

Fortunately the time difference between Carramer and California was only two and a half hours, so Caroline was able to place a call to her twin right away. Eleanor sounded surprised to hear from her so soon. "I thought you'd be too busy soaking up all that royal attention to call," she said.

"I am, Caro," Caroline said carefully, using the form of her name they had agreed on as a code word to indicate that all was not well. "The flight was perfect and I can't fault the warmth of the prince's welcome, or his hospitality. The suite he has allocated to me is quite sumptuous and larger than the ground floor of our house."

"Then what's the problem? Enjoy yourself."

Eleanor sounded as if she meant to hang up, so Caroline said quickly, "Didn't you hear what I said, *Caro?*"

"I heard you, *Eleanor,*" her twin returned with equal emphasis, sounding far from pleased. "Surely it's too soon for you to be having second thoughts about your engagement to the prince?"

"This whole idea is a mistake. I hate lying to Michel,"

Caroline said, lowering her voice although it was unlikely she could be overhead through the thick walls of the palace. In the adjacent bedroom a maid was unpacking her cases, but the activity sounded sufficiently muted to reassure Caroline that her conversation was equally private.

"Has Michel turned into an ogre since last we saw him?" Eleanor was being deliberately obtuse.

"You know he hasn't. He's as charming as we remembered. More so, if anything." Too late, Caroline heard the betraying huskiness in her voice.

Eleanor seized on it immediately. "I'll bet you're afraid you'll fall for him if you go through with this."

Caroline was glad her twin couldn't see her face. Her voice had already given away too much. "How I feel is beside the point. I'm simply not a good enough actress to keep this up for much longer."

Eleanor's laughter rippled over the line. "It sounds to me as if your only problem is liking Michel more than you anticipated. Where's the harm in that?"

The harm was that nothing could come of it as long as he was legally bound to her sister, Caroline thought despairingly. "I still think you should come and settle this matter as we agreed," she appealed.

"And I will, as soon as Danny and I are officially engaged. It may happen soon because I've been booked at short notice for a modeling assignment in Las Vegas. The model they originally hired is ill. Danny has arranged to take a few days off to come with me, so we can spend my free time together. I'm certain he intends to propose while we're there."

Caroline's heart sank. She might have known something like this would happen. "How long will the assignment last?"

"Four days, but we'll stay longer if Danny can get

away." There was a pause when Eleanor seemed to be waiting for Caroline to say something. When it lengthened,
Eleanor said, "You don't begrudge me a holiday, do you?
We both need a vacation, and this way each of us gets to
have one without breaking the bank."

It was all very well for Eleanor, Caroline thought. She
didn't have to pretend to be someone she wasn't and she
could allow her feelings for Danny full rein without wor-
rying about the consequences. She controlled her temper
with an effort. "When do you plan on coming to Carramer?"

There was another long pause. "Maybe I won't have to
come at all if you sort things out with you-know-who."

"Did you ever intend to come?" Caroline couldn't resist
asking.

"Of course I did." Eleanor sounded affronted at the implied accusation. "But now you're there and Michel has
accepted you, there doesn't seem much point in me turning
up and confusing the issue."

"What about my work?" Caroline asked, wondering if
her twin had planned this from the beginning. "I can spare
a couple of weeks away while business is quiet, but I can't
keep this up indefinitely."

Eleanor laughed again, dismissing Caroline's concern.
"You won't have to. If Michel looks like he'll be getting
you anywhere near the altar, simply tell him the truth and
he'll send you packing so fast you probably won't even need
a plane."

It was exactly what Caroline didn't want to happen. The
thought of Michel's reaction when he found out how she'd
deceived him made her want to curl up with remorse. But
she had agreed to keep up the deception until Eleanor was
safely engaged to Danny and she would do it. She only
hoped it wouldn't be for much longer. "Call me from Las

Vegas as soon as you know where you're staying," she asked.

"I will. You'll be the first to know when Danny's ring is on my finger," Eleanor promised. "Wish me luck."

Caroline was the one who needed luck, she thought, but murmured the expected words anyway. When Eleanor hung up, she felt more alone than she had in a long time.

She decided to take Michel's advice and rest after the journey. The maid had finished unpacking for her and had turned down the massive four-poster bed in anticipation of her needs. But although Caroline slipped off her clothes and stretched out on the cloud-soft bed, sleep eluded her. She kept seeing Michel's face as he quizzed her about Caroline's activities. She couldn't help thinking that he had seemed more interested in Caroline than in catching up with his supposed fiancée.

After an hour of tossing and turning, Caroline felt less rested than when she had lain down. So she got up, indulged in a cool shower in the ornate marble bathroom of her bedroom, then changed into one of the outfits Eleanor had chosen for her. It was comprised of a black Lycra bodysuit with a black-and-white Polynesian-print sarong-style skirt tied over it and a sheer black-and-white georgette shirt left unbuttoned to function as a jacket.

In deference to the balmy weather she limited her makeup to a sheen of lightly tinted moisturizer, some lip gloss and Eleanor's clear mascara. Her hair had settled down a little during her nap, so she brushed it into a compromise between her own relaxed style and her twin's tousled mane.

Although Eleanor's clothes were more stylish than Caroline's normally casual choices, she had to admit that they made her feel smarter and more ready to face Michel again.

Depending on how she felt, she could have afternoon tea brought to her room or join the prince on the lower terrace for afternoon tea, the maid who had unpacked for her had informed her. Too restless to stay in her suite any longer, she opted for the latter and set off in search of the prince.

As a child she had only visited the more public areas of the palace, so inevitably she got lost in the maze of rooms and corridors. Twice she had to ask members of Michel's staff for directions and twice she got lost trying to follow them, until she found herself facing a set of French doors opening onto the garden. At least they led outdoors, she thought in relief. Once outside she might be able to get her bearings more successfully.

Instead of leading to the landscaped gardens sloping away from the palace toward the sea, the doors opened on to a walled garden where tropical plants, native palms, ferns and figs created a tranquil haven. As soon as she stepped out and the French doors whispered closed behind her, the call of unseen birds reached her from high among the branches and her senses were teased by a potpourri of tropical fragrances from stands of gloriously colored Carramer orchids.

She paused, uncomfortably aware that this was a private garden, perhaps Michel's own retreat from the demands of royal life. She didn't wish to intrude. The prospect of retreating into the maze of corridors and galleries she'd just left didn't appeal either, so she took a few tentative steps forward. "Hello, is anyone here?"

There was no reply, then the sound of childish giggles caught her attention. She headed along a narrow gravel walkway toward the source of the sound, coming to a halt at a grassy clearing. At its center was a wooden playpen with a baby inside piling colored blocks one on top of another. When the tower was three blocks high, the baby tumbled them over by accident or design, dissolving into peals of laughter at the destruction.

She crouched beside the playpen. "I don't suppose you know the way back to the terrace?"

"Can I help you, Miss Temple?"

The sound of her name brought Caroline's head up. The baby had distracted her from noticing an attractive young Carramer woman on a swing seat nearby, a magazine open on her lap. Setting the magazine aside, she approached Caroline and offered her hand. "Hello, I'm Shona."

"Pleased to meet you, Shona," Caroline said as she shook the woman's hand, adding curiously, "How do you know my name?"

The young woman smiled. "The staff were briefed to expect you today, Miss Temple. Is there something you need?"

This level of attention would take some getting used to, Caroline thought. When she explained about being lost, Shona nodded. "The palace can be confusing at first. I'll have someone show you the way."

Before she could do so the baby began to make complaining noises at being ignored. He had stopped his game and was gazing at Caroline with soulful eyes, his pupils huge and dark in his sweet face. The baby tumbled onto all fours and moved crablike toward her, before levering himself up by the bars of the playpen and reaching out two chubby arms.

"You seem to have made a friend," Shona observed.

"May I?" When Shona nodded her permission, Caroline lifted the infant into her arms, inhaling the clean, powdery scent of him as she adjusted her position to let him ride comfortably on one hip. Living in so many native villages until her teens had given her ample opportunity to handle babies of all ages. For some reason they were equally drawn to her.

A baby magnet, Eleanor had called her teasingly, warning

Caroline that it would be different when she had babies of her own. "Then you don't get to hand them back."

Unlike her twin, Caroline didn't find the thought bothersome. She would be far more disturbed if she thought her future didn't include children of her own. The baby gurgled happily as she jiggled him up and down. She turned to Shona. "What's your baby's name?"

A frown darkened the young woman's face. "He's not…"

"His name is Luc."

Michel's sudden appearance caught Caroline by surprise. Equally surprising was the way her senses went on alert the moment he filled her field of vision. With the baby in her arms she felt curiously vulnerable and hoped he wouldn't notice as he scrutinized her with maddening slowness.

Her body's febrile reaction to his closeness made her uncomfortable, but she couldn't seem to do anything to control it. The spicy scent of his cologne competing with the orchids was a further assault on her peace of mind, making her wonder if Eleanor was right. Was she regretting the deception because she feared she was finding Michel far too attractive already?

The sight of Eleanor cradling the baby brought Michel up short. She looked like a Donatello painting of Madonna and Child, he thought. After her rest, her hair had softened somehow and it flowed around her heart-shaped face like a silken waterfall. His fingers itched to tangle with it, to discover if it was as soft to his touch as it looked.

The strength of the impulse caught him by surprise. After reading about her in the magazine, he had almost expected to dislike the woman she had become, inviting her as much to satisfy his curiosity as his brother's decree. Now he found himself revising his opinion of her. The self-centered and slightly hard woman quoted in the article seemed a world away from the gentle, sweet creature he had welcomed this morning.

With the baby in her arms she looked, why, lovable, he thought. Another surprise and, this time, a dangerous one. They might be betrothed, but he had no intention of falling in love with Eleanor—or anyone else for that matter. If they married, and it was an oddly appealing idea at this moment, it would be on his terms. All the same, he found himself gripped by a sensation very like jealousy as he watched baby Luc curl tiny fingers into the inviting cleft between her breasts. His reaction made him frown.

Seeing Michel's flinty gaze and a certain tightness around his eyes, Caroline sensed that he wasn't pleased to find her in his private domain. "What are you doing here?" he asked, confirming her suspicion.

"I was coming to join you for afternoon tea and lost my way," she said.

Before she could apologize for her unwitting intrusion, he said, "Next time, I'll assign someone to bring you to me."

His tone, that of a royal decree, made Caroline's hackles rise. She was jet-lagged and on edge with the strain of pretending to be someone she wasn't. It didn't help to find herself fighting an attraction she had no business feeling. He might be the prince, but Eleanor was supposed to be his fiancée, not his captive. "Wouldn't it be easier if I ask the kitchen for some bread crumbs and leave a trail of them whenever I leave my suite?" she flung back at him.

His sensual mouth twitched, but his face remained impassive. "It might be easier, but it's a lot messier and bad for the Persian carpets. I don't recommend it."

The baby in her arms began to squirm and thrust his fist into his mouth. "I think little Luc is hungry," Caroline said, welcoming the distraction. Michel mad at her was bad enough, but at least she could give as good as she got. Michel teasing her in response was more than she was ready to deal with.

He took the baby from her, cradling it easily against one shoulder, apparently unworried by the possibility of damaging his expensive shirt. She knew her mouth was open in astonishment and was even more annoyed when Michel seemed to find her reaction amusing. "You didn't expect a prince to be adept with babies?"

Stung at being read so easily, she shook her head. "I imagine you get plenty of practice at kissing babies when you're out among your people."

"You're confusing princes and politicians," he pointed out. "I haven't had much practice, but I picked up a few things from playing with Lorne's two."

She had known quite a few men who relished the role of uncle, but few of them were as natural with infants as Michel appeared to be. He didn't object in the slightest when Luc gathered up a fistful of elegant peaked collar and began to chew on it. "You're right, he is hungry," he said indulgently and gestured to Shona hovering in the background. "Would you take him inside and see to his food?"

Shona sketched a curtsy. "Of course, Your Highness. Would you like some tea sent out?"

He nodded. "It's cooler here than on the terrace." He turned to Caroline. "Are you comfortable here or would you rather go inside?"

Being in the open air with him was infinitely preferable to sharing an enclosed space where his size and air of masculinity risked making her feel even more vulnerable, so she shook her head. "It's lovely out here."

He looked at the baby in his arms. "Luc seems to agree with you."

She tickled the infant under the chin and he laughed in delight. "He's adorable. What is he—eight months old?"

"Nine," Michel supplied. He handed the baby to Shona with obvious reluctance, and as the young woman took the baby inside, Caroline noticed how his eyes followed them. A strange prickle crept up her spine. Was there something between him and Shona? She told herself she shouldn't let herself be influenced by his reputation as the playboy prince, but the thought persisted. It shouldn't be any concern of hers, but Caroline was bothered by the thought nonetheless. Telling herself it was on Eleanor's account didn't lessen the feeling.

Michel's gesture invited her to join him on the swing seat Shona had recently vacated. Shared with his substantial frame, it felt too small for comfort and the gently rocking motion made it difficult to keep some distance between them. Whenever her bare leg brushed his trouser-clad thigh, a jolt like a miniature electric shock went through her. "Is Shona Luc's mother?" she asked, wanting to keep some conversational distance at least.

"She's his nanny. Luc's mother died shortly after his birth."

Caroline's mother had also died of complications following the twins' birth, and her heart went out to the little boy. She looked at Michel, unable to conceal the mistiness in her eyes. "What about his father?"

A long moment passed before Michel said quietly, "Luc is my son."

Her heart did a quick dance, and she felt the color drain from her face as the rumors about the playboy prince spun through her mind once more. Her fantasies about Michel didn't include him having a child by another woman, and it troubled her more than she would have believed possible. He had said that Luc's mother was dead. Had he loved her?

If she had lived would he have married her? What would have happened to the betrothal then?

She tried to tell herself that none of it concerned her. She was Eleanor's proxy, nothing else. But the twisting sensation in her stomach suggested a more personal interest in Michel's past. In his present, if she was honest. She shouldn't care how many women he'd been involved with, but it was hard not to be, when she had held the proof of his love in her arms only moments before.

She hadn't held it against the baby. To Caroline's way of thinking, Luc was innocent and beautiful, like all babies. Closing her eyes, she recalled the warmth of his body curled against her, and the stomach-clutching sensation of having his tiny fingers curled around her breast. When Michel sent Luc inside with the nanny, Caroline had felt a surprising sense of loss.

There was loss involved in her feelings for Michel, too, she recognized. Given his reputation, it shouldn't come as a surprise to find he had fathered a child by another woman, but it did. It was probably just as well, she told herself. It would stop her from putting him on some sort of princely pedestal where he didn't belong. From the moment she had seen him again at the airport, her fantasies had been in danger of getting out of hand. Luc was probably the reality check she needed, although she had trouble making herself believe it.

Michel's closeness on the swing seat was wreaking havoc with her thinking processes, but she wasn't sure how well her legs would support her if she tried to stand and move away. She tried to look unaffected and suspected she failed miserably. "You're Luc's father?" she repeated as much for herself as for him. "I'm not sure I understand."

A flicker of amusement played on his handsome features. "What don't you understand? His conception? His birth?"

She felt a blush start but fought it. "That isn't what I mean. I'm not so naive that I don't know where babies come from," she snapped back. "I mean, how could this happen when you're officially betrothed to El…to me?"

"A betrothal is not necessarily a love match."

And his affair with Luc's mother was? Caroline dragged in a breath that only half filled her lungs. Had he loved Luc's mother so much that marrying a stranger to whom he had been betrothed in boyhood was preferable to risking his heart again? The thought was acutely painful, but it made sense.

At the same time she realized that her pain had as much to do with her own recent past as with her feelings for Michel. Ralph's actions had made her feel as if she was second-best and now she felt it again. As Eleanor's stand-in, Michel's love life shouldn't make any difference to Caroline, but she couldn't shake off a renewed sense of betrayal.

"I see," she said heavily. "What am I doing here, Michel?"

His sharp breath hissed between them. "In the interview you gave the magazine, you said you preferred to marry for money and position rather than love because you've had enough of poverty, traipsing around the world with your father. My people expect me to marry, but I'm not looking for love, either. So we seem ideally matched. As I can offer you everything you say you want, I assume the old contract between us is mutually beneficial."

So she was right. He had loved Luc's mother and, having lost her, was only prepared to marry for appearances' sake. It was what Caroline had begun to fear since Michel told her Luc was his son, but having it put into words felt like the clash of doom. The irony was, her twin would have agreed with Michel until she met Danny O'Hare-Smith and discovered that she could marry for both love and money.

"Magazines work several months ahead. I could have fallen in love with someone since that interview," she said, striving unsuccessfully to keep her tone light.

"Official duties aside, there's no reason my wife can't enjoy the same freedom I claim for myself, provided we're discreet, naturally."

"Naturally," she murmured, amazed that he sounded so matter-of-fact. It might be how a royal romance was conducted, but it argued against everything she believed marriage was about. "You're talking about a marriage of convenience," she said, finding the words hard to force out.

"Am I?" He asked so softly that she wasn't sure she'd heard right.

Her shocked gaze went to his face and she regretted it immediately as she saw her own desire reflected back at her. Heat surged deep inside her, ignited by his smoldering gaze. Her heart did a quick double beat, and she swallowed hard. "Surely you can't have it both ways?" She told herself she was asking on Eleanor's behalf although it felt more as if she wanted to know on her own account.

"Do you honestly think we can have a marriage of convenience, given the sparks that have been flying between us since you got off the plane this morning?"

She shook her head, unwilling to acknowledge the truth of his assertion. The betrothal was between him and Eleanor, but Caroline was the one sharing his sexual tension. She couldn't entirely suppress it, but she could refuse to give in to it. "You're imagining things."

"There's one way to find out." Anchoring the swing with one foot on the ground, he slid his arm around her shoulder and pulled her against him in a sinuous movement. Try as she might to fight it, she felt sensations of pure pleasure flow through every inch of her body, pooling at the center of her being.

As his mouth hovered above hers she caught her breath, knowing she should end this but finding herself enthralled by his scorching gaze. His moves were smooth, as if he'd had a great deal of practice at seducing women. She didn't want to be one of them, but with her bones turning rapidly liquid, she knew if he meant to kiss her she wouldn't have the strength or the will to stop him.

To her astonishment he limited himself to brushing her lips with his, although it was enough to send white fire racing along her veins. Her ragged breathing told him everything he needed to know and he regarded her with satisfaction. "You see, I am right."

His closeness threatened what little peace of mind she had left and she jumped up, paced to a flame tree and rested her palms against the cool, cinnamon-scented bark. "I can hardly challenge a royal prerogative, can I?" she said, annoyed at betraying herself so thoroughly. "The penalty is probably losing my head." In more ways than one, she realized.

He looked amused. "If I had invoked royal prerogative, you wouldn't be over there while I'm over here."

She crossed her arms over her slender body, although the gesture wasn't much defense against the images his words burned through her mind. "You're moving too fast for me," she admitted, not sure to whom.

He frowned. "Isn't fifteen years long enough to wait?"

"You didn't wait."

She hadn't meant to say it, but she was glad she had, for Eleanor's sake, she told herself hastily. Michel's relationship with Luc's mother was none of her business, but it nagged at her like a sore tooth she felt compelled to probe repeatedly, regardless of the potential for pain.

He slid fluidly out of the swing and came closer but didn't touch her. His nearness felt as compelling as a touch and was more disturbing for being embellished by her imagination. "Are you jealous of my past relationship with Luc's mother?" he asked quietly.

As Caroline, the answer came to her instantly but she throttled it back, forcing herself to voice the one Eleanor would have given. "Of course not."

"Just as well, given your romantic history," he murmured, and she saw tension seep out of him, as if he had been bracing himself for some reason.

Caroline's own past would give Michel no cause for jealousy, she thought furiously. Her unwillingness to sleep with Ralph had been part of their undoing, she was well aware. He hadn't understood—hadn't wanted to understand—that she saw her virginity as a gift she could only bestow once, and she wanted the occasion to be truly special. It might make her a dinosaur in this liberated time, but if she had learned anything from her eccentric father, it was the importance of choosing your own path.

For this reason, Caroline didn't think any less of Eleanor for doing things her way. Growing up in so many diverse cultures, Caroline had happily learned to live and let live, although she sometimes wondered if Eleanor's many affairs had made her happier than Caroline's self-imposed celibacy. It didn't always look that way. Now, however, it had created another problem.

"I suppose you're referring to what I said in the interview?" When the prince nodded, she tossed her hair the way Eleanor would have done. "Surely you don't believe everything you read in magazines?"

"I believe my eyes," he said flatly. "You are beautiful and sexy, and I imagine you're accustomed to using it to get your own way. Fortunately, Carramer society takes a realistic view of women. These days they are no longer expected to remain dewy-eyed virgins until they marry.''

She and Eleanor had toyed with flaunting Eleanor's past as proof that she wasn't remotely suitable to marry Michel. They had dismissed it because Caroline hadn't felt able to carry it off. Now it seemed that it wouldn't have worked anyway. On to Plan B, Caroline thought, wishing she had a Plan B. ''Would it change things if I was already married?'' she asked.

His eyes narrowed. ''Of course it would. But enough of this. My security people assure me you aren't married, or planning to be.''

She felt her face flush and hoped Michel would blame it on the warmth of the afternoon. ''Why should I? You said yourself, everything I want is right here.'' The honesty of the statement caught her by surprise, but she made an effort to mask it.

He searched her face and seem satisfied. ''I think you mean it.'' Then his expression hardened. ''In any case, there will be no opportunity since you'll be remaining in Carramer until our wedding.''

''You mean I'm to be a prisoner here?''

''An honored guest, under royal protection,'' he demurred. ''As my future consort you could become a target for terrorists or kidnappers. Carramer is safer than many places, but we live in dangerous times.''

The greatest danger was in front of her, she thought, wondering how much palace security it would take to protect her from herself. The way she was starting to feel toward Michel made staying a reckless proposition. All the same she was glad she hadn't let Eleanor walk into this mess. Even if Michel kept Caroline in his palace till the cows came home, he couldn't force her to honor a contract that didn't concern her. The thought should have cheered her, but to her chagrin, it had the opposite effect.

She clung to one conviction. Eleanor must not come to Carramer and put herself under Michel's jurisdiction. It would be far better if she simply eloped with Danny and presented her marriage to Michel as a fait accompli, then there would be nothing the prince could do about it.

Caroline felt chilled, imagining his anger when he found out. Even as a boy, Michel had liked to win. He mustn't win this time, she told herself grimly. She wouldn't either, but hadn't expected the knowledge to hurt this much.

Chapter Three

"I might have known the Aquarium would be on your itinerary," Caroline said with a laugh. Marine creatures had fascinated Michel since boyhood, and Caroline knew from his sister's letters that Michel's patronage had helped to make the Aquarium at Aviso one of the finest in the world.

The prince frowned. "I realize fish don't turn you on, Eleanor, but I thought you'd appreciate a break from meeting officials and touring their offices."

"You're right, I do." Caroline forced lightness into her voice although the condemnation in his tone stung a little. As Eleanor, she was supposed to prefer nightclubs and restaurants to beaches and coral reefs. For Caroline herself, the opposite was true. She hated being cooped up in crowded places with strobing lights and music that jarred her teeth, much preferring the wonders of nature.

She preferred being outdoors at any time, and this morning's tour of Michel's administration had sorely tested her patience. She had admired the handsome new parliament house with its lush tropical gardens and felt genuine interest in the work of the government officials to whom she was introduced, but she was glad when it was over and welcomed the change of scene far more than Michel could know.

Equally troubling was the deferential way she was treated everywhere they went. She hated lying to Michel and his people, even by omission, but what else could she do if she was to buy her twin as much time as possible?

Caroline chewed her lip. Pleading jet lag had enabled her to stave off the tour for a couple of days, then Michel himself had become tied up with official business, so nearly a week had passed since she arrived on Isle des Anges.

Eleanor should have called from Las Vegas by now, but there was still no word, and without knowing where her sister was staying, Caroline had no way to get in touch with her.

At least Eleanor was in the right place to arrange a quick marriage, Caroline thought. Preferably not a ceremony presided over by an ersatz Elvis, she mused, but a small, dignified wedding that would put Eleanor beyond Michel's reach forever.

Sadness enveloped Caroline as she pictured Eleanor marrying Danny in Las Vegas. As teenagers they had dreamed of attending each other's weddings, planning their gowns and ceremonies down to the last detail. They had never considered a double wedding, Caroline thought. Every bride was entitled to her own special day. She had just never imagined being on the other side of the ocean on her twin's wedding day.

She pushed the sadness away. Seeing Eleanor pressured into an arranged marriage would be even sadder. Her future happiness depended on Michel continuing to believe that Caroline was his fiancée. She didn't have to like it. She only had to keep it up for a short time longer.

The thought helped her to relax a little, outwardly at least, as she followed Michel into the Aquarium. It was a tranquil oasis with enormous tanks recreating the famous reefs that ringed Isle des Anges and attracted scuba divers from around the world. After the bright tropical sunshine, the dim coolness came as a relief.

"I hadn't realized how hot it was outside," she murmured.

He shot her a concerned look. "If the heat troubles you, we can return to the palace."

She shook her head. Coping with her increasingly complicated feelings toward him was easier when they were on neutral ground. "There's no need. The Aquarium staff have obviously gone to a lot of trouble to prepare for this visit."

Seeing him regarding her in evident surprise, she frowned. "Is something wrong?"

"Apparently not. If you are sure you're quite well, we shall continue with the inspection." At the prince's signal, the Aquarium director began to lead the royal party through the displays.

Michel only half listened as the director described how water was pumped directly from nearby Turtle Bay to provide a natural environment for the vast collection of tropical fish, sea snakes, eels, shell fish, sharks and sponges.

As the Aquarium's patron, Michel had heard it all before so he felt entitled to let his thoughts wander. What was going on here? Eleanor had not only grown more beautiful with the years but apparently more compassionate as well. Twice today he had glimpsed her stifling a yawn as she toured the administrative complex, but only when she thought no one could see her. In public she had been the model of attentiveness and interest. She was obviously feeling the effects of Carramer's tropical climate, but she had opted to continue the tour rather than disappoint their hosts.

Pretending to inspect a tank of rare emperor cod, he studied her reflection in the glass. Her hair swung around her shoulders in a silken curtain, more becoming in his opinion than the contrived style she had worn when she arrived and that she evidently preferred in her modeling work. This look was much more to his taste, he decided. It practically invited him to swirl his fingers through it.

She was also more simply dressed in white silk pants and a coral-colored shell with a white summer jacket draped around her shoulders, the effect stylish but hardly couture. He massaged the back of his neck with one hand. It was as if there were two sides to Eleanor's personality. When she stepped off the plane, she had looked every inch the up-and-coming model. Then he'd found her cradling the baby in his private garden and she had seemed more caring and vulnerable, a very different person from the self-centered Eleanor he had known years before.

The grown-up Eleanor awoke in him feelings he hadn't anticipated and didn't want. If she kept on being so pleasant, he knew he could start to care for her. A wave of desire curled through him as powerful as it was unexpected, and he clenched his fists until the nails dug into his palms. He had meant it when he said theirs would be no marriage of convenience. The chemistry between them was far too powerful. But making love to her was one thing. Loving her was quite another.

He was too aware of the misery his brother had endured in his first marriage. Under their law, if fate hadn't intervened, Lorne could have been in that hell for life. Yet Lorne had stubbornly refused to legalize divorce, even for himself. Was it any wonder that Michel was gun-shy? He accepted that his position required him to marry, but he intended it to be on his own terms.

When he made Eleanor his wife, it would be with the

understanding that she had no claim on his heart. Not now, not ever. He would provide for her, and she would give him as many heirs as his position required. Other than that, his life would remain his own.

The plan had seemed ideal when Michel first conceived it. Now he was astonished at the turmoil it created inside him. He watched a pair of sea snakes undulating through the water behind glass a few inches from his face, their movements as fluid as his thoughts. All his life he had been sure of his position in life and what was expected of him. When had that changed?

He grinned wryly to himself. He could practically pinpoint the minute. It had happened when he saw Eleanor walking toward his limousine at the airport. Her grace and beauty had taken his breath away. He hadn't expected her to be as sweet as she was lovely and he hadn't a clue what to do about it.

The sea snakes coiled together, their intentions unmistakable, and he felt overheated suddenly. He wanted Eleanor more than he would have believed possible. The very thought of what they would share after they were married sent a rush of blood through him, and he had to look away from the tank.

That brought his gaze back to Eleanor. She listened intently as the director explained how divers went into the tanks each day to feed the larger fish. Her round eyes and troubled expression suggested she found the idea daunting. He would have to teach her to swim with sharks, Michel thought. Once she knew them as fellow creatures, she wouldn't be afraid of them.

He didn't want her to be afraid of anything in his kingdom, he thought, especially not him. If he couldn't allow himself to love her, at least he could offer her companionship and the home she'd always yearned for.

"Sir?"

He wrenched himself back to reality. The others were waiting for him to move on before they could continue the tour. He made his feet track, wishing they could cut this short and return to the open air. He felt overheated and short of breath, which was odd, given that he kept himself in peak physical condition. Finding Eleanor at his side, her hip brushing his, didn't help. In fact, he'd swear it was the cause of his discomfort.

She smiled at him and his heart turned over. "The Aquarium is magnificent, Michel. You should be proud of what you've accomplished."

He couldn't help smiling back even though he was puzzled. "My, how you've changed."

A frown creased her forehead. "I have? How?"

She seemed alarmed at the idea. Personally he was delighted. "As a child, you complained that fish were cold and slimy and watching them made you shiver."

Her laughter sounded slightly forced. "How could I ever have made that mistake? They're so beautiful. Their colors remind me of living rainbows."

Michel wondered at her reaction, as if she disliked being reminded of the child she had been. He could understand it. In those days, it had seldom occurred to her to consider the feelings of others. She much preferred getting her own way and hadn't been above charming others into giving it to her. Hearing her echo his own belief was strange but he found it heartwarming. "Wait until you see the Living Coral room."

He exchanged a few words with his aide and the tour swung toward a separate room lit by ultraviolet light. When they entered, he was rewarded by Eleanor's cry of delight. "It's amazing."

He had been here many times before, but seeing it

through her eyes was like the very first time. The director fell silent as Michel launched into an impassioned description of the various types of coral that glowed luminous under the special lights. After a few minutes he realized what he was doing and cut off the lecture, his features uncomfortably warm.

"I didn't mean to get carried away," he said softly to Eleanor.

She dismissed the apology with a touch of her hand on his arm, her expression radiant in the eerie light. She looked as excited as he felt. "Everyone should have a passion for something. With me it's flowers."

Too late, she realized that she had spoken as Caroline, but thankfully Michel didn't seem to notice. "All the same, not everyone needs to hear the entire story of the nautilus shell since prehistoric times. Promise you'll tell me if I start to bore you again?"

She laughed. "Very well, but I wasn't bored this time and I'm not likely to be."

It was true, she thought. Whether Michel spoke of his plans for his people or his passion for the undersea world, she found his enthusiasm infectious. In an era when it was almost fashionable to remain unmoved about anything, he didn't mind letting his enthusiasm show. Nor did he stop at lip service. The world-class aquarium itself was proof of his willingness to commit his time and energy to a cause.

He was a remarkable man, she thought. Born to a life of wealth and privilege, he had no need to exert himself over anything beyond his official duties. Yet he chose to devote himself to many interests and causes. The director had confided that the prince wasn't above donning a wet suit and going into the shark tank to feed the huge creatures by hand.

A shiver shook her, and she knew it was because she had trouble thinking of him going into danger. It wasn't fair to let herself feel this way when nothing could come of it, but Caroline couldn't stop her chest tightening as she imagined him swimming alongside the man-eating sharks, his lithe black-clad body inches from their gaping jaws.

Needing the reassurance of his living presence, she glanced up to find him watching her curiously. Had he seen her shiver? She hoped he would blame it on the coolness of the atmosphere.

"Would you like to leave?" he asked softly.

"Any time you're ready," she said blithely, trying to become Eleanor again. She wasn't sure how well she succeeded.

Evidently Michel was fooled. "You know what you used to tell me. When you've seen one fish..."

"...you've seen 'em all," she finished as Eleanor, wishing he didn't sound so disappointed in her. She couldn't help adding, "I enjoyed the visit, though, honestly."

"The staff evidently think so and that's what matters," he said, sounding unconvinced on his own account as he led the way back to the waiting limousines. Soon they were settled against cool leather and bathed in conditioned air, with a partition providing privacy between them and the driver.

Michel released a sighing breath as he relaxed visibly. How rare these moments were for him, she thought. It must be a strain always having to be on display for other people, never able to let tiredness or boredom show. No wonder he kept a private garden at the palace where he could be himself.

He broke into her thoughts. "You made quite a few fans today."

Michel wasn't one of them, she read between the lines. As a child, Eleanor had never pretended to find nature as fascinating as Caroline did. She was sure he was remembering those times, believing her enjoyment to be an act. She yearned to assure him that her enthusiasm was genuine, but she couldn't do it without arousing suspicion so she let the troubled silence lengthen.

He misread her mood. "My apologies if the tour went on too long for your liking."

"As your wife I'll have to get used to doing my duty, shan't I?" she snapped back, her anger fueled as much by hurt at being so badly misunderstood as by the need to sound like her twin.

"As my princess you will have your share of official duties, but I'll try to make sure they aren't too onerous. Unless you're referring to your *wifely* duties," he added with a touch of haughtiness.

She challenged his look with one of her own, hiding the desolation coiling through her at the thought of him with a wife. Surely Caroline wasn't picturing herself in the role? Rejection colored her tone. "Perhaps they're the ones I'll find most onerous."

He gave a scornful laugh. "I sincerely doubt it, but I'm happy to put your mind at ease on that score."

He slid an arm around her shoulder and angled his lean body across her so she was effectively trapped. She couldn't restrain a gasp as his thumb gazed her lower lip and another shiver racked her, this time from pure pleasure.

For a woman as experienced as Eleanor, she reacted with almost virginal rapture when he touched her, Michel thought. Under the half-closed lids her pupils were huge and dark, and a rose flush colored her skin, reminding him of the fragile coral in the aquarium.

When his mouth closed over hers, shock parted her lips, and he wasted no time in accepting the implied invitation, allowing himself to explore her mouth with a thoroughness that would have melted a statue.

She was no statue, and he could feel her practically melting under him. As he tantalized her delectable lips, he let his hands wander over the womanly fullness of her body. For a model she was remarkably curvaceous, but just enough and only in the right places, he decided. He had always believed that models had to starve themselves to meet some ideal of thinness and he was pleased to discover that Eleanor didn't subscribe to the practice.

He had intended the demonstration to be for her benefit while he stayed cool and in control, but he was amazed at how quickly fire tore through his body. She had a way of kindling it, as if he was a taper and she was a flame. Flames burned, he reminded himself, but it didn't stop him from deepening the kiss.

The temptation to take more than a kiss almost overwhelmed him. He was a bit old to be necking in the back of a limousine, but she made him forget where he was, even who he was, and that a sheet of soundproof tinted glass was all that separated them from potential scandal. He forgot everything but how warm and silken her sun-kissed skin felt and the way she trembled under his hands. Virginal. The word crept into his mind again. She responded as if a man's touch was a novelty to her, but it couldn't be. She had admitted as much in print, sounding proud of her conquests.

He could hardly lay claim to monk status himself and he wasn't hypocritical enough to subscribe to the old double standard, yet reading about her attitude toward men had unsettled him. She had suggested that she chose her partners according to some shopping list of money, status and power.

Was that how she ranked him? The thought should have pleased him. He had fallen in with his brother's wishes because Eleanor also seemed to want a marriage that left them both free to pursue their separate interests.

Now, as he caressed her and pressed his lips to the slender

column of her neck, he felt her pulse flutter as he tasted the satiny skin with his tongue and his neat plan rocked beneath the intensity of his own needs. He felt like a dormant volcano, awakened by some cataclysmic event over which he had minimal control. He had no way to measure how long the explosion would take to come, but unless he put some emotional distance between them, come it would.

She wanted this, Caroline admitted to herself. Michel's mouth on hers was exquisite torture, expertly demanding intimacy of a kind she had never experienced before. She had certainly never wanted to give a man as much of herself as she gave to the prince in the kiss. Her anguished pleasure ignited her passion as she realized that this was all she could ever have of him.

She shouldn't be kissing him at all, far less enjoying it, she told herself in panic. She had never meant the deception to go this far, but she had no idea how to control the torrent of responses he invoked. The way his mouth claimed hers and his breath filled her was so fiercely possessive as to be utterly irresistible.

She was seized by a longing so deep it was akin to pain. She knew where it came from. More than anything, she wanted to be loved, and to have a home and a family of her own. Michel's kiss taunted her with how it could be, all the more bittersweet because it was a fraud. Even if the betrothal contract had been made with her instead of Eleanor, he didn't intend to love any woman the way she wanted—no, ached—to be loved. He preferred to fulfill his duty as husband and father in public while claiming his freedom in private.

He didn't want a wife. He wanted a harem, she thought bitterly. She tried to be glad she was here instead of Eleanor, so her sister didn't have to deal with this, but it didn't stop her from feeling bewildered and she knew it was on her own account. Crazy woman, she derided herself. *You knew what you were getting into.* At least she thought she had, until her response to Michel's touch began to confuse the issue.

"No," he murmured, pulling away from her. "I don't think you'll find your wifely duties onerous at all."

She wanted to slap him, partly because he was right. If she had been betrothed to him, the prospect of their wedding night would have filled her with excitement. His kiss amply demonstrated how easily he could arouse her. She blushed to think just how easy it had been. She had no doubt he knew how to satisfy a woman as well. But his skillful seduction only emphasized that he was anything but a one-woman man. It didn't help that her body had its own ideas and had no problem with his skill at all.

"Would you like to return to the palace and rest?" he asked as coolly as if the turbulent kiss hadn't happened.

Perhaps it was different for him, she thought as disappointment flooded through her. To her searching gaze his expression was closed, his eyes dark and unreadable. She knew she had few skills as a lover, inexperience being the main reason, but it had never bothered her as much as it did at that moment. Against all common sense she wanted his expression to echo the wonder and excitement he had made her feel. When she found nothing, she could only conclude that there was nothing to find because it was all on her side.

Eleanor would have forced more of a response from him, Caroline felt sure. Her twin often dissected her lovers' faults and virtues in a way that made Caroline feel for the men involved. Eleanor had even offered to teach Caroline what she called "a few moves," but Caroline had insisted that she would know what to do when the man and the time were right. She had always believed that. Now she wasn't so sure. If she had listened, perhaps Michel wouldn't have released her so readily as if, having tasted his fill of her, he was ready to move on.

She was unable to dismiss his effect on her so easily. Her heartbeat raced, her pulse pounded and her cheeks felt flushed and those were only the physical effects. The mental ones were much more subtle and dangerous. She had never come so close to regretting her lack of experience before. Michel was starting to get under her guard, she realized in some trepidation. Returning to the cloistered confines of the palace seemed rash until she had herself under better control.

"I don't need to rest, I'm fine," she assured him, striving to mask her hurt and disappointment behind an Eleanor-like coolness. She saw his eyes narrow and felt a little better. Why should she give him the satisfaction of seeing how disturbed she was that his kiss had swamped her personal defenses, while leaving him apparently unscathed?

"Something to eat, then?" he proposed. "You may recall that Anges is renowned for its local produce."

Food was the furthest thing from her mind at that moment. Feeling as she did, she doubted if she could force anything down as long as he was close enough to touch. "Don't you have some…some princing to do?" she asked in desperation.

A smile tugged at his generous mouth. "Trying to get rid of me, Eleanor? It won't work. I intend to stay close to you until our wedding day."

"I'm surprised you want to marry me at all if you trust me so little."

He shook his head. "On the contrary, I trust you implicitly—as long as you are under my eye."

That hurt, although in Eleanor's case, it was not wholly unwarranted. "You have a country to run. Surely you can't be at my side every minute until we're married?"

"Not every minute," he agreed gravely although she got the distinct impression that he was laughing at her. "I do, as you put it, have a good deal of princing to do, and royal duties are not great respecters of personal privilege."

She was intrigued in spite of herself. "So what will you do, clap me in irons when you can't keep an eye on me?"

He gave a theatrical sigh. "Unfortunately, the dungeons at the palace haven't been used for a couple of centuries so they're much too dank, not to mention supposedly haunted."

She shuddered as imagination took hold. "Thank goodness for small mercies."

A dark eyebrow canted upward. "You don't think I'd really consider locking you up until our wedding? Carramer may have some quaint traditions, but that isn't one of them, so relax. I have a much better way to keep you out of mischief."

"Just about anything would be better than a dungeon," she said, intrigue overcoming her chagrin at being tagged as a potential troublemaker. "What is it?"

"You'll see when we return to the palace," he promised. "I recall that patience was never your strong suit, but it's a useful attribute for a princess to develop."

"Patience is a useful attribute for anyone," she agreed, earning a raised-eyebrow look. It tempted her to add, "Especially considering the nature of the prince she has to deal with."

"Careful," he cautioned. "*My* patience is not unlimited."

"In my country we call it 'sauce for the goose,'" she quoted, wondering what imp of mischief drove her to taunt him. She was playing with fire, but she couldn't seem to stop herself. It was the need to get a reaction from him, any reaction, she sensed. Even the annoyance she saw in his gaze now was better than the indifference he had shown when he kissed her.

He frowned. "I believe the entire expression is, 'What is sauce for the goose is sauce for the gander.' Are you threatening me, Eleanor?"

She pretended innocence. "Who, me? You're the one who wants a marriage that's no marriage at all. If that isn't 'sauce for the gander,' I don't know what is."

She sounded bothered by the prospect. Truth to tell, it had begun to bother Michel, too, far more than it should. For some reason the idea of her claiming equal right to have discreet affairs after they were married had lost much of its appeal. He wasn't sure it was what he wanted for himself anymore, either. Could a week really make so much difference?

In the company of the right woman it could, he concluded. Maybe his brother was wiser than Michel gave him credit for. Perhaps he had seen in Eleanor some quality that Michel had overlooked. Could she be the right woman for him after all?

Had the playboy prince finally met his match? The sobering thought preoccupied him as he escorted Eleanor into one of the island's finest resort hotels where their party was expected for lunch.

Chapter Four

Caroline's spirits sank when she heard her twin's recorded voice on their answering machine for the third time in as many hours. Her own messages sounded increasingly desperate, but she simply had to get in touch with Eleanor and she couldn't until she knew where in Las Vegas she was staying. She could only record another message on their machine at home and hope that Eleanor had the sense to check it occasionally from wherever she was.

Caroline had debated whether to start calling Las Vegas hotels at random, but there were too many. A visitor's bureau might have known where Eleanor's photographic crew were working, but the shoot was only due to last four days. By now Eleanor would be vacationing with Danny among the tourists thronging the popular destination. Caroline had no idea where to start looking for her.

By the time she returned from lunch with Michel, she knew she couldn't go on deceiving him for much longer. Already his kisses threatened to drive her over the edge of reason. She might not affect him as strongly, but for her he possessed all the dangerous appeal of forbidden fruit.

It had begun years before when they were children. He had beguiled her with his humor, charm and intelligence. As an adult, she had felt sure she could control her response to him. Instead she found herself on a roller coaster of emotions, driven to the heights of passion one minute and plunged to the depths of despair the next.

She was glad that Michel believed she was Eleanor, but it hurt that he didn't seem to like what he saw. Her twin was no Goody Two-shoes, but Eleanor needed to be self-centred and ambitious to succeed in her chosen profession.

One call wasn't asking too much, was it? Caroline glared at the telephone. When it remained stubbornly silent, she faced facts. Eleanor was avoiding her for fear Caroline would try to pressure her into coming to Carramer. If she only knew, it was the last thing on Caroline's mind. Once on Carramer soil, Eleanor would be subject to Michel's rule, bound by local law to marry the prince. Only by marrying Danny before Michel discovered the deception could the trap be avoided.

Knowing they had outwitted Michel should have comforted Caroline, but it only added to her despair. Once he found out, she wouldn't be surprised if he never wanted to see her again.

She wouldn't blame him, but that didn't mean she would feel any less hurt. It was bad enough to have him kiss her and remain cold and unmoved. Having his indifference turn to outright rejection was a blow she knew she wouldn't recover from quickly.

Her sigh echoed around the lavish suite. Even Ralph's flagrant infidelity hadn't managed to dent her self-esteem as much as Michel's imperviousness to her kiss. It wasn't only her pride, although goodness knew that had taken a beating.

It was realizing that she couldn't make him feel what she felt. Had he set out to prove that he could be a husband in every sense without love coming into it? It might be his idea of the perfect marriage, but it struck Caroline as a recipe for lifelong misery.

Just as well she wasn't really his fiancée, she told herself. She could never be the sort of wife he wanted, filling a role rather than a place in his heart. Eleanor might have managed it if she hadn't been in love with Danny. Caroline was suddenly glad for her twin, overruling the siren song of jealousy her heart wanted to sing. During the last few years she had worried that Eleanor might marry for money or position and live to regret it. Now that worry was gone.

A baby's cry interrupted her thoughts. She went to the French doors and stepped out onto a balcony overlooking the garden. Shona was on the path beneath, pushing Luc in his baby carriage. The young nanny saw Caroline and smiled. "We're going to feed the swans. Would you like to come?"

Caroline nodded. "I'll be right out."

Seeing how much Caroline enjoyed the baby's company, the nanny had taken to including her in their afternoon outings. The gesture touched Caroline, especially now when she felt so alone. Michel might be indifferent to her, but his son appreciated her, she thought with faint reproach.

The feeling was mutual.

"How's my little friend today?" she said, tickling the baby under the chin with one finger. Luc blew her a raspberry and laughed in delight. "I guess that means he's in good form," she said to Shona.

The nanny nodded. "It's such a glorious day I thought we'd spread a blanket on the grass by the lake. Luc loves watching the swans."

They walked on in companionable silence until they

reached a lagoon where black swans glided against a back-drop of cascading water from a small waterfall. Caroline couldn't suppress a pang when the baby held out his arms to be picked up. When she obliged, he babbled contentedly and reached for the charm she wore on a fine gold chain around her neck.

Shona disentangled his fingers and he began to protest but relaxed when she gave him a rattle to distract him while she settled him on the blanket in the shade of an ironwood tree. Caroline dropped down beside him and curled her arms around her bent knees feeling some of her tension ebb away as she watched the baby investigate the toy with total absorption.

Suddenly he held it out to her and her heart turned over. "For me? Thank you, Luc." She accepted it with a huge smile that made him laugh in delight. When she shook the rattle playfully in front of him, he reached for it again and she gave it back, feeling a pang grip her as his baby fingers with their tiny, perfect fingernails tangled with hers.

Something caught inside her, a need strong enough to rob her of breath for a moment. The smallest leap of imagination could make Luc her baby. She fought the drive to make it so. Luc belonged to Michel, his love to Luc's mother. Even the right to marry the prince belonged to someone else.

Impossible situation. She was caught between wanting Eleanor to come to Carramer herself and dreading the possibility, when Caroline would be truly redundant here.

She hid her agitation as Shona sank to her knees with the grace common to Carramer women. "I've seen you wear the Mayati before," the nanny said, indicating the charm. "How did you come by it?"

The Mayat were the earliest-known inhabitants of Carramer, reaching the islands by sea from the Philippines and Indonesia two thousand years before. Fragments of their jade work were still being unearthed on the remote islands. Most prized were the fingernail-size charms called Mayati that had been exchanged as tokens of respect at births, marriages, funerals and other ceremonial events. The modern-day inhabitants valued them for their craftsmanship and the belief that they gave the wearer particular blessings.

Caroline fingered her own bird-shaped token with its tiny shell eye. "I lived in Solano as a child, and a teacher gave it to me for good luck when I left. She also gave my twin sister one, but hers is in the shape of a turtle."

Shona looked pleased. "A turtle means she will be blessed with many children."

Caroline wondered what Eleanor would think of that. "The bird means health and long life, doesn't it?"

Shona hesitated. "It has several meanings, health and long life being one. Some believe it promises happiness with a man."

"You mean I'll have a happy marriage?"

Shona looked away. "Not marriage exactly. More like—" she searched for the right English word "—pleasure."

Understanding dawned, suffusing Caroline's features with warmth. She had treasured the Mayati for its association with a place she loved, rarely taking it off. Exploring its implications hadn't occurred to her, and she was sure her teacher hadn't known its more colorful possibilities either.

Not that she was superstitious, but living among so many primitive cultures gave her a healthy respect for other people's traditions. Now, remembering Michel's effect on her, it was tempting to see a connection. She fingered the Mayati thoughtfully, realized what she was doing and let the charm drop back against her throat. After today's demonstration, pleasure was the last thing she wanted to associate with him since it was so obviously one-sided.

During lunch he had been cool and distant. Did he regret kissing her? It hardly suited his wish for a show marriage with no strings attached. She looked at Luc who was gurgling happily as he lay on his back exploring his toes. Where did the baby fit in with Michel's plans?

He was obviously devoted to his son, spending time with Luc every day and reading to the baby at bedtime every evening, even if he had to excuse himself from a state dinner to do so.

If fatherhood wasn't the problem, then a wife was, she concluded. "Why is there no divorce in Carramer?" she asked in impulse. "Or is this the only place on earth where all marriages end happily ever after?"

Shona shook her head. "Sadly, it isn't. Mistakes are made, especially by the young. But with no way out, the law has the effect of making us…how do you say it? Look before we leap. As a result we have far fewer unhappy marriages than most other countries."

Including her own, Caroline thought soberly, remembering the grim statistics. "What about royal marriages?"

"They are expected to set an example."

"I heard that Prince Lorne had an unhappy marriage. Couldn't he change the law or something?"

Shona looked troubled. "Our ruler is a very just man. He would never change laws to suit himself. Although rumor has it that he was unhappy, he remained faithful to his wife until she died in a car accident. Now he has the beautiful Princess Alison as his consort."

Fate wouldn't always be so opportune, Caroline thought. She was starting to understand why Michel insisted on some ground rules for his own marriage. They ensured that he gained the wife his position required without risking a repeat of his brother's experience. Eleanor's free and easy attitude toward marriage meant she would have been content with the bargain, too, if Danny hadn't stolen her heart first.

Thinking of her twin reminded Caroline that they still needed to talk. With luck, there would be a message from Eleanor waiting for her by the time she got back to her suite.

But the only message was from the prince, reminding her that she was to dine with him and a guest that evening. He didn't mention who the guest was, but it was probably another Carramer government official. Yesterday it had been the minister of justice.

Caroline made a face. She had nothing against justice, but this gentleman risked giving it a bad name. He was utterly prejudiced and argumentative. Several times when she had opened her mouth to retort, she had caught Michel's warning glance across the table and had subsided into mutinous silence.

If this was how Eleanor was expected to behave, she wouldn't have lasted five minutes as a royal bride, Caroline couldn't help thinking. Keeping her opinions to herself had never been one of her twin's virtues. It wasn't especially one of Caroline's, but she was at least inclined to count to ten before speaking out.

If she couldn't voice her opinions, she could at least express them in her appearance, she decided with a sudden flaring of rebellion. She dismissed the maid who came to help her dress and indulged in a long soak in the huge marble bathtub, scenting the water with a fragrant liquid she found alongside it.

With her hair dressed in an upswept style she had seen Eleanor wear, she applied her makeup a little more dramatically than usual, paying extra attention to her eyes. The result was startling, she decided, inspecting herself critically. She didn't quite match Eleanor's sophistication but she did look glamorous, she thought in slight astonishment. She *never* looked glamorous. Of the twins, she had always been ''the natural one.'' The plainer one, she thought on a sigh.

Well, not tonight.

All the same she felt a few misgivings as she slipped on one of the cocktail dresses Eleanor had packed for her. It had a body-hugging bodice in a midnight blue color flaring to a ballerina-length skirt of cream taffeta. A confection of chiffon spilled over her shoulders and down her arms, leaving her throat bare and exposing what felt like a huge amount of décolletage.

She had intended to take off the Mayati, but some imp of mischief made her leave the charm where it was. So it ensured pleasure, did it? She wondered if Michel would recognize its more obscure meaning or if he would care.

She knew what was going on here. By remaining indifferent to her, Michel had dented her pride and she wanted to get even. Without conscious intent she had dressed with the express purpose of arousing him so she could have the satisfaction of returning his indifference in spades.

She moved to a cheval mirror and turned this way and that, biting her lip. There was an awful lot of her on display. Then she lifted her head, pride refusing to let her back down now. If he remained indifferent to her dressed like this, he must be made of stone.

He wasn't, she saw when she joined him in the salon for a drink before dinner. Royal practice enabled him to suppress all but a flicker of emotion, but by now she was sufficiently in tune with him to catch his narrowed eyes and the muscle working at his throat, a reaction that she guessed would amount to agitation in anyone less skilled at disguising their feelings in public.

A thrill of pride coursed through her. She had done it, moved the unmovable. It didn't feel as satisfying as she thought it should.

He looked marvellous in a white dinner jacket that enhanced his wide shoulders and dark pants that made nonsense of her image of him as a stone man. Hard, tough, honed to physical perfection maybe, but never stone. Not when the clothes adjusted to his lithe movements as if made of some viscous liquid instead of fabric. Hastily she shifted her gaze to his face.

Big mistake. The flinty look in his eyes made her wonder if he was aware of her strategy. Later for you, his look seemed to promise. She swallowed hard, wondering if she had bitten off more than she could chew.

"What would you like to drink?" It was said civilly enough, but a faint steely undertone threaded his voice.

She glanced at his drink and shuddered delicately. She had never liked spirits. "Champagne, thank you."

The prince signaled to a servant hovering in the background and a goblet of French champagne was proffered on a silver salver. She took it and the servant bowed and left. "It must be nice never having to lift a finger," she said tautly, wishing the servant had stayed. Suddenly she wished she hadn't chosen tonight to be provocative. Michel's kiss was still vividly imprinted on her lips, and his gaze went to them as if he was remembering it, too.

The look gave her pause for thought. Was he as unaffected by her as he had made her believe? Then she made herself remember his icy withdrawal. After the first burst of passionate connection, she had looked into his eyes and found...nothing. No desire, not even warmth. He had shut himself off from her, making good on his vow to give her her due as his wife, without allowing his emotions to become involved.

Michel raised his glass in a toast, the gesture somehow mocking. "You look stunning tonight, Eleanor. Much more your usual self."

Warily she sipped the champagne. "I'm not sure I understand."

"Since you arrived, there have been moments when I suspected you of playing a part."

She almost choked on the champagne and set the crystal goblet down before it slid out of her suddenly nerveless fingers. Had he guessed her true identity? "I still don't know what you mean."

"Don't play the innocent with me. Until this evening you almost had me believing you'd changed your spots.'

Her mind whirled. What had she done to give herself away? There was nothing for it but to admit the truth. "I wondered when you'd work it out," she began.

Before she could go on he cut the air with a slashing movement of his hand. "It wasn't difficult. I've been deluding myself that the self-centered child I once knew had grown sweet and compassionate as well as beautiful. But that was the act, wasn't it? What did you hope to gain by trying to make me think you'd changed?"

"Nothing," she said with a touch of bitterness. It was small consolation to find he hadn't guessed the truth after all. His derision was much harder to deal with.

His eyes narrowed. "Nothing but the satisfaction of twisting me around your little finger, don't you mean? Is that what your ego demands, Eleanor? The men in your life falling at your feet in helpless adoration?"

"I'd be wasting my time expecting it from you, my prince," she said bleakly, thinking of his cold response to her kiss.

He moved closer and touched a finger to her chin so she was forced to tilt her head to meet his disdainful gaze. "If you had accepted that, we would be making progress. Somehow I think you will require more convincing before you give up your pointless power game."

She tried to summon a laugh. When that failed, she settled for trying to breathe when all the air in the room seemed to be gone. For a moment she wished she *was* Eleanor, who could have shrugged off his nearness with a flippant remark instead of feeling this terrifying pressure around her heart. The nearest Eleanor-like response Caroline could manage was a feeble, "What do you have in mind?"

He gave a throaty laugh, but its coldness chilled her. "You tempt me to answer that by carrying you off to my chamber and making love to you until the stars shift in their movements."

She gasped as he dragged her against the rough wall of his chest. His hand against her back felt fiery through the chiffon of her dress. A gush of pure, savage desire ripped through her, catching her unawares. She was appalled at herself for feeling such a response when he clearly felt only contempt toward the woman he thought she was. It didn't halt the tremors gripping her. "You wouldn't," she whispered, not sure whether it was a protest or a plea.

"Make no mistake, I would if I thought that's what it would take to tame you. My reputation as the playboy prince is not entirely unearned," he warned. "But I won't because it's exactly what you want me to do. Your whole demeanor this evening, even that Mayati around your pretty neck, is designed to drive me to my knees with desire for you, isn't it?"

At her indrawn gasp he smiled without humor. "Oh yes, I recognized the charm the day you arrived wearing it. Let me see. The polite story is that it brings the wearer good health and long life. The much older and not-so-polite interpretation is that it guarantees sexual pleasure. Were you hoping it would work its magic until I gave you what you so obviously want and became your willing love slave?"

She clutched a hand to the charm. "Of course not. I only found out today that it has another meaning."

His eyebrow canted upward. "I think you really expect me to believe you. You remind me so much of Chandra."

To her dismay he set her aside effortlessly and returned to the side table where he'd left his drink. His hand was rock steady when she knew she couldn't have picked up the champagne glass without dropping it to save her life. Another demonstration of how easily he turned her on while remaining unmoved himself, she thought with bitter self-reproach.

"Aren't you going to ask me about Chandra?"

"She was one of your lovers, I imagine." Amazing how the word stuck in her throat.

He shook his head. "She was my brother's first wife, a foreigner like you, and she thought the sun rose and set around her."

Caroline remembered Shona mentioning Prince Lorne's unhappy first marriage. It galled her to be compared to such a woman. "What happened?"

"She thought being married to my brother gave her the right to behave as she pleased, enjoying the privileges of being royal without accepting any of the responsibilities. She was driving too fast over a road she had been warned was dangerous when she lost control of her car and it was all over."

The lesson wasn't lost on Caroline. Michel had no intention of tolerating such a marriage, but Caroline knew that even Eleanor was incapable of behaving with such selfish abandon. The marriage would never happen as long as Caroline had breath in her body, but she felt perversely driven to defend her twin's honor. "Just because your brother had a tragic marriage, it's hardly fair to condemn your wife in advance," she said on a note of defiance.

"You of all people should know what they say about love and fairness."

"Doesn't that quotation mention something about war, too?"

His steady gaze impaled her. "Is that what this is, Eleanor? If it is, I warn you it's a war you cannot win. Give up this futile attempt to turn our marriage into a power struggle, and I will give you a life of ease and comfort. You can have anything your heart desires."

"Except a claim on you."

"Except that," he repeated heavily. "Is it such a terrible bargain? A life of royal privilege in exchange for a marriage that doesn't put either of us in chains?"

He made it sound civilized, she thought. Before she met Danny, Eleanor would have had no difficulty accepting the arrangement. Caroline herself was the one with the problem, and there was no way Michel would ever marry *her,* so why did her heart feel like a stone inside her chest suddenly?

"Maybe we should end this betrothal here and now before somebody gets hurt," she suggested.

Michel sighed. "It is not so simple. Under Carramer law, the bargain our fathers made is binding on us."

"Then unbind it. You *are* Carramer law. You can dissolve the contract." She felt her eyes narrow. "But you don't want to, do you? This arrangement suits you just fine." His expression betrayed him, and she added tonelessly, "Well that makes one of us."

"Are you so certain? Your response when I kissed you, and now when I took you in my arms, tells me you need no Mayati to find my attention...pleasurable."

The slight catch in his voice made her look at him in surprise. "That also makes one of us." If he felt desire for her on a level such as he made her feel for him, he masked it spectacularly well. She was astonished how much the awareness hurt.

Michel felt his jaw tense. Putting some emotional distance between them had seemed like a good idea at the time. He was surprised that she seemed to be hurt by it. Her pride was probably wounded. Accustomed to bringing men to their knees with her beauty and sensuality, she didn't know what to do with a man she couldn't manipulate. Good. He didn't want to hurt her, but she needed to understand that what she wanted was precisely what he wasn't prepared to give her.

He wouldn't allow any woman to control him. That way lay madness. He had seen it in his brother when Lorne fell under Chandra's spell. Schooled from birth to rule the country, Lorne had always been so strong, so in control. It had torn something inside Michel to see his brother at the mercy of his late wife's manipulations. If that car crash hadn't intervened…

Strange how hard it was to think about even now. According to Lorne, his second wife, Alison, made him happier than he had ever been and Michel was glad for him. But he couldn't help remembering Lorne's misery with Chandra and wondering what the odds were for a truly happy marriage. Maybe he should spend more time with them and see if it rubbed off, Michel thought ruefully until he remembered why he chose to stay away. Nothing had changed there.

Eleanor had changed. The thought intruded unbidden, resisting his attempt to dismiss it. He had seen enough, felt enough to know she was capable of deep passion and caring. If he allowed himself to love her, he could bring those qualities out in her, encourage her to drop the brittle mask that he was starting to suspect was a survival tactic and to become for all time the sweet, compassionate woman he had so far only glimpsed.

No. The denial exploded through his mind. Lorne had made that mistake with Chandra. Bewitched by her, he had thought she would change after they married and it hadn't happened. It never did. Michel forced himself to deal with what was, not what could be. Perhaps Eleanor had developed a thick skin as a result of her unusual childhood, but it wasn't up to him to change her. Keeping his emotional guard up was still the best course.

"I never claimed to love you," he said, irritated by the effort it took to keep his voice even. "Our marriage is not conditional on either of us being or falling in love, but on fulfilling a mutual contract."

"Wrap her up and I'll take her with me," she said, sounding bitter. "You make it sound like a business deal."

Her pain-filled tone tugged at him, but he kept his arms rigidly at his sides, although they ached to enfold her and soothe the hurt away. "Royal marriages are frequently akin to business deals," he said carefully. "As long as both parties have something to gain, I see little wrong with it."

"Of course not. Your image benefits from having a wife and family at home, while you indulge yourself in affairs whenever you feel like it. The best of both worlds."

It sounded far less attractive spilling from her delectable lips like an accusation, he thought. "Isn't it what you want?" he demanded, provoked in spite of himself. He felt his features tense. "Or is there a secret romantic underneath your brittle exterior? Are you dreaming of being carried over my threshold into a life of cozy domestic bliss?"

Her expression betrayed her for a split second before she masked it with disdain. "You've made your conditions clear. The one thing I learned in my travels with my father was the wisdom of not wishing for the moon."

Her bleak tone undermined some of his certainty. He had been so sure that they both wanted the same kind of marriage. No strings. The best of both worlds, as she described it. Was he wishing for the moon, too?

Could he marry her and not become emotionally involved? His very thoughts suggested it would be a struggle. "We agree that a romantic marriage is wishing for the moon," he told her tautly. "A pragmatic arrangement is far less likely to wither and die with the years."

"Romantic love doesn't automatically wither and die," she snapped, sounding defeated. "One partner or the other has to kill it through deliberate cruelty or neglect."

He ached to go to her and soothe the pain he heard in her voice but held himself back with an effort of will, limiting himself to saying, "As your husband, I will never deliberately be cruel to you, nor will I neglect you. You will want for nothing that is in my power to give you."

She knew perfectly well that cruelty wasn't in Michel's nature. She remembered his gentleness as a boy when he had rescued an injured seal pup and nursed it back to health before releasing it into the wild. Even now, if he turned over a seashell to examine it, he carefully replaced it in position to avoid harming the creature inside.

Neglect wasn't one of his flaws, either. Despite the heavy burden of his royal duties and responsibilities as governor of the island provinces, his baby son was far from neglected. Michel had also spent far more time escorting Caroline around than was good for either of them.

Still he heard what he avoided saying—that love was not in his power to give her. She fingered the Mayati at her throat. Why couldn't it have promised her wedded bliss instead of physical pleasure? Surely the last was meaningless without the first?

In horror she realized where her thoughts were going.

Now who was wishing for the moon? She wasn't going to marry Michel so his attitude to love hardly mattered to her. She was an impostor. As soon as he found out how she had deceived him it would be all over. She would be on the first plane out of Carramer and she would never see him again.

All the same, she couldn't resist asking, "Is this what you plan to teach Luc as he grows to manhood?"

She had touched a chord she saw when his eyes clouded. "Luc will learn that royal privilege has its price."

"A price you see yourself paying now, by marrying out of duty instead of love?"

He passed a hand briefly across his eyes. When he dropped it, his expression was impassive. "This is a futile discussion, Eleanor. We have a saying in the islands. 'What is, is.' There's no point wishing things were different when they can't be—wishing for the moon, as you put it."

She hugged herself in an unconsciously protective gesture. "If a prince can't have what he wants, what hope is there for the rest of us?"

His long, slow look seared her. "The prince will have what he wants, even if not in the way you feel he should want it."

It was the first admission that he wanted her—or the woman he believed she was. The effect on her was incredible. Her breathing became shallow and her whole body trembled as she imagined them together. She had already tasted his mouth, felt his caresses and everything in her cried out for more.

She sank onto an antique chaise, feeling as if her legs wouldn't hold her for much longer. Reaching for the champagne, she managed to sip a few drops. Instead of steadying her, the drink weakened what little resolve remained. If he came to her now, she knew she was lost.

But he stayed where he was, a picture of rigid control in

contrast to her own turmoil. She must have managed to hide most of it from his searching gaze because he didn't react to the unsteadiness of the glass in her hand. Had he even noticed? She should be grateful for small mercies, but she felt contrarily cheated that he didn't take advantage of her momentary weakness. Some people were never satisfied.

A servant appeared at Michel's elbow and murmured a few words to him. "Regretfully we'll have to finish this *intimate* discussion another time. It seems our dinner guest has arrived," he informed her after the servant withdrew.

"Who is it?" she asked, torn between relief at the interruption and agitation at knowing they weren't finished yet. A third person at dinner would be a welcome buffer between them, but she had no interest in who it might be. Her thoughts were too ragged and confused. Given the way she felt now, Michel would be lucky if she managed to make lucid conversation with his guest.

All that changed as soon as they entered the dining salon and she saw who it was. "Vava Rose," she exclaimed in amazement. She shot a questioning look at Michel and saw that he looked insufferably pleased with himself. "But where...how..." The sight of the woman, once so dear to her, robbed her of speech momentarily.

The woman stood up and smiled. "Please call me Isola. Vava was appropriate when you were a child and I was your teacher, but there's no need for titles between us now. It's so good to see you again, *ma amounou*."

The Carramer endearment, commonly used to indicate the special relationship between a mother and daughter, was all it took. The years fell away and Caroline went into Isola Rose's open arms, feeling her throat tighten and her eyes mist. If things had been different, they could have been stepmother and daughter in reality.

Isola had welcomed the twins into her private school as

if they belonged on Carramer, treating them exactly as she treated her other pupils. To Caroline, feeling as if she belonged somewhere was such a novelty that she had embraced it wholeheartedly, singing the teacher's praises whenever her father would listen. He had been sufficiently intrigued to meet Vava Rose—Isola, Caroline amended her thoughts. Something had clicked between them. They had begun seeing each other whenever August could tear himself away from his research, and he had eventually proposed marriage to the teacher.

Caroline's pain warred with her joy at the reunion. She knew because it had been explained to her that much soul-searching had gone into Isola's decision to turn August down. She hadn't wanted to leave her beloved Carramer and August had been too restless to stay anywhere for long.

Caroline's arms tightened around the teacher, noting that she was still slim and beautiful despite the passing years. "I remember you as being taller," she murmured, hearing the catch in her voice.

Isola laughed, hearing it, too. "I remember *you* as being smaller. Let me look at you." She held Caroline at arm's length, her sharp blue eyes taking in every detail. "You've grown into a beautiful woman, Caroline."

A frown darkened Isola's features, then her face cleared and she smiled self-deprecatingly. "Of course. You two were always so alike that I had—mouth, telling you apart. Evidently I'm no better at now than I was when you were in my school."

"They may still look alike, but they're very different in personality," said—Eleanor?

She nodded, knowing he didn't even has a contribution. Her sense of humor reached a high. "These days I'm a model and Caroline is a fiery designer."

Chapter Five

Caroline's heart lurched and her breathing threatened to stop. Isola always had been quick. As a child, Caroline had suspected that the teacher had eyes in the back of her head, so unerringly had she homed in on any untoward behavior on her students' part. Could she possibly have seen through Caroline's imposture so quickly?

Michel spoke first, amusement coloring his tone. "I'm afraid you've got the wrong twin, Isola. This is Eleanor, not Caroline."

A frown darkened Isola's features, then her face cleared and she smiled self-deprecatingly. "Of course. You two were always so alike that I had trouble telling you apart. Evidently I'm no better at it now than I was when you were in my school."

"They may still look alike, but they're very different in personality, aren't you, Eleanor?"

She nodded, knowing he didn't mean it as a compliment. Her sense of unease receded a little. "These days I'm a model and Caroline is a floral designer."

Isola turned to Michel. "They haven't changed that much, Your Highness. When they were children, Eleanor liked to show off and Caroline enjoyed making me pretty things with flowers."

At a signal from Michel, they moved into a small, informal dining room where a round table made of ironwood was polished to a gleaming patina and set with pristine table linen and jade-handled silverware. Candles flickered in tall silver holders. The dinnerware was made of china so fine it was almost translucent, engraved with the royal crest.

At any other time Caroline would have enjoyed the sense of luxury, especially after spending so much of her childhood in places where facilities like running water and sanitation were luxuries. But seated between Michel and Isola, she couldn't shake off a feeling of impending doom. She was imagining things, she told herself. Lots of people still confused her with Eleanor. Just because Isola had made the same mistake didn't mean the woman suspected anything.

The feeling subdued her appreciation for the first course of paper-thin salmon marinated in pineapple wine, but she ate to avoid arousing suspicion. When Isola made no more reference to her identity, Caroline chided herself for allowing her fears to overwhelm her joy at seeing Isola again. "I still can't believe it's really you," she admitted when their plates were being whisked away.

Isola's hand slid over hers. "Believe it, honey. There's only one of me in the whole of Carramer, and many people think that's one too many."

"They must be former students who never saw your softer side," Caroline admitted with a laugh. When Isola had disciplined her or Eleanor for some misdeed, they had been among the people wishing her to the farthest reaches of the islands, but as they came to know her outside school hours, Caroline especially had come to love her as the mother she had never known. Seeing her now brought back so many happy memories that a lump lodged in her throat.

"It took you two long enough to admit I had a softer side," Isola said tartly. "When you came to my school, you were as undisciplined a pair as I'd ever met. Comes of growing up in wild places with a father who's more interested in dead cultures than living daughters. How is August, by the way?"

The warmth in Isola's voice belied the criticism of her father, Caroline noted, wondering if the teacher still carried a torch for her former suitor. Maybe there was still hope for the two of them. She stifled it. Their relationship hadn't worked out before. There was no reason to think it could work out now. "He's been out of touch for a while, living in a village along the Amazon, studying the remains of a culture that used to worship snakes. If I know Dad, he's having the time of his life."

Isola sniffed loudly. "Typical. If he ever gets back to civilization, I wouldn't mind hearing from him once in a while."

"I'll tell him—when I see him," Caroline promised, not sure when that would be. "But what about you? Did you ever marry? Do you still have your school?"

"No to both questions. I'm sure you know that your father is what you call a tough act to follow. The school is still going, but it's in younger hands now. When Prince Michel heard that I planned to retire from teaching, he invited me to become cultural adviser to his court."

Caroline's gaze flickered to the prince who had so far kept out of the discussion. He waited until a footman silently replenished their glasses with vintage champagne, then twirled his glass between thumb and forefinger. "Isola's invaluable to me as an adviser on foreign cultures and introducing our cultural traditions to visitors."

"Which is where you and I come in," Isola added. "His Royal Highness tells me you need a refresher course in Carramer language, history and traditions to prepare you for your coming marriage."

Remembering Michel's vow to provide her with a watchdog when he couldn't keep an eye on her personally, Caroline felt robbed of some of the pleasure of seeing her friend again. She was sure Isola had no idea of the real role Michel had chosen for her, believing she was here purely as a tutor. "His Royal Highness has thought of everything, as usual," she remarked, keeping her tone level although the look she directed at him should have frosted the champagne in his glass.

He lifted it in a mocking toast. "You're welcome, my dear."

"So you'll be as proficient as possible by your wedding, when we're together we'll speak only Carramer," Isola continued briskly, ignoring the charged atmosphere around her. "We can start as soon as His Royal Highness wishes."

"You see," Michel said, his tone laced with irony, "with Isola to take care of you, you won't have time to be lonely or homesick."

Since arriving she had been neither, she thought in some surprise. In fact her sense of being at home in the islands had grown from the moment she landed at Aviso Airport. It was only Michel himself who prevented her from feeling completely at home, and she shied away from examining the reasons too closely.

None of them were Isola's fault. "I'll enjoy working with you," she assured the older woman. "My Carramer is pretty rusty, but with you to help me, I should pick it up again in no time."

"Then your ability must have improved since you attended my school," Isola said with some asperity. "Unless you've somehow caught Caroline's gift for languages. Still, we will work with what we have.''

Caroline almost winced as Isola's phrase brought back memories of attending her school. ''Working with what you have'' was one of the teacher's maxims, she recalled. Caroline wondered how the phrase applied to this situation.

Michel looked pleased. He was enjoying himself, Caroline thought furiously. He had chosen his watchdog with care, selecting the one person she would never willingly hurt. The high regard the twins held for their former teacher made sure of it, a fact he had known because she had discussed it with him when they were children.

Bewildered by the romance between her father and the teacher, she had cornered Michel and asked him if it meant they would finally settle down and have a real family life. Michel had gently advised her not to get her hopes too high, pointing out that her father had been on his own all their lives and might not be willing to change. As it turned out, Michel had been right. So he knew precisely how Caroline felt toward Isola and she was furious to think he wasn't above manipulating her to get his own way.

Again she was thankful that Eleanor hadn't walked into the trap, although it bothered Caroline to think there was no escape for her.

Imagining again Michel's reaction when he found out the truth, Caroline clenched her hands beneath the table. What would he do? So far his preferred method of punishment was to take her in his arms and kiss her senseless. The very thought sent the blood racing through her body and her heart into overdrive.

That was for misdemeanors like arguing with him. His reward for deceiving him was unlikely to be so... pleasurable, she thought. The word lingered in her mind, a vivid reminder that his kisses were the sweetest torment she had ever experienced. No other man made her feel the way Michel did, balanced on a knife edge between pleasure and pain, wanting him yet fearful of the power of her own desire.

Then her father's motto came back to her. "Act with honor and you'll be welcome anyplace on earth." She could practically hear his gruff voice in her ears and sense his disapproval of her actions. Goodness knew, he had good cause, even if he didn't know it. She could hardly claim to be acting honorably toward Michel, no matter how she justified it.

When had it started mattering so much? Michel was no saint. He had no intention of letting her leave until the betrothal contract was fulfilled, so she should be glad she had outwitted him. Instead she felt more alone than ever.

She made herself pay attention to Isola. If she really had been Eleanor, the lessons would have been a vital part of her marriage preparations. Languages had never been Eleanor's forte, although Caroline had picked them up easily. How long would it be before Isola noticed the difference?

This had already gone on too long. She would get in touch with Eleanor if she had to do it by smoke signals, Caroline resolved. She jumped as a traditional Carramer dish called *fruits de mer* was placed before her. It consisted of crab and lobster in coconut cream with cassava and banana, cooked in banana fronds that were then opened like flowers on the plate to reveal the delicacies within.

Michel caught her startled reaction. "Don't you like this dish? I'll have something else brought for you."

She stopped him with a hand on his arm. "It's one of my favorites, truly. I was miles away, that's all. I guess I'm still not used to being waited on hand and foot."

Touching him was a mistake, she realized as awareness

seared along the nerve endings from her fingers all the way to her brain. Afraid a fast retreat would betray her inner turmoil, she withdrew her hand slowly. Breathe, she ordered herself, striving to ignore the play of sculpted muscles under her trailing fingers. Neither attempt was entirely successful.

As she removed her hand, Michel released an audible breath, making her wonder if he shared her tension. The only outward sign was a slight tightening around his generous mouth, but it could just as easily indicate disapproval. Lord knew, he'd shown enough of it toward her since she arrived.

Toward Eleanor, Caroline reminded herself. Whether Michel felt desire or disapproval made little difference when neither was meant for her.

Instead of cheering her, it depressed her in ways she didn't want to think about. She made an effort to do justice to her meal and hold up her end of the conversation. If nothing else, it saved her doing too much thinking.

"I tried to get in touch with you soon after I arrived," she told Isola. "But I was told you'd moved from your old address."

"You didn't have to wait until now to get in touch. A letter now and then would have been nice. I wrote to you and your sister."

Caroline fastened her gaze on her plate. "I know. We lived in such wild places that the mail sometimes took months to catch up with us. Sometimes it never did." She didn't add that writing to Isola reminded her painfully of what might have been.

Isola seemed to sense it anyway. "You would have liked to stay, wouldn't you, *ma amounou?*"

My daughter. If only…

Several heartbeats passed before Caroline could summon

her voice. "Of all the places we lived, Carramer was where I felt most at home."

"And your sister?"

About to admit that Eleanor preferred the excitement and fast pace of city life, Caroline caught herself in time. "She loved Carramer, too."

"But not enough to return with you?"

She knows, Caroline thought again, her agitation rising. She fought it. If Isola was suspicious, panicking would only confirm her suspicion. Beside Caroline, Michel stirred slightly as if waiting for her reply.

"She intends to come as soon as she can get away from her work." It was close enough to the truth to serve.

"Does she still wear the Mayati I gave her?"

Automatically, Caroline's hand went to the charm at her throat. "Like me, she seldom takes it off. Back home I'm often asked about the significance of mine."

"And do you tell them?" Michel drawled, his tone challenging.

She wanted to hit him. She had no intention of embarrassing her former teacher who she was sure had chosen the charm for its commonly accepted blessing of good health and long life. She still wasn't convinced that its connection with sensual pleasure wasn't a myth. She couldn't deny the effect of Michel's embrace on her, but his experience as a lover was a more likely explanation than the power of an ancient jade charm.

She was saved from having to answer when a footed crystal bowl was placed in front of her. "I haven't eaten strawberry guava in years," she said a touch overbrightly to conceal her relief.

"It is known as the fruit of lovers because it is bittersweet," Michel volunteered a little dryly. He waved away his own serving and stood up. "Excuse me, ladies. I shall look in on Luc briefly but return in time for coffee. Please finish your meal. I'm sure you have much to catch up on.''

Alone with Isola, Caroline pushed her half-finished dessert aside. She wasn't surprised when Isola said, ''Why are you pretending to be Eleanor, Caroline?''

Caroline let her gaze drop. ''How did you guess?''

''So it's true?''

''Yes.''

Isola sighed. ''When Prince Michel corrected me the first time, I hoped I was wrong. I suspected it as soon as I saw you wearing the bird Mayati I gave to Caroline, instead of the turtle I chose for Eleanor.''

Again Caroline's hand flew to her throat. So the charm had given her away. She hadn't thought to swap with Eleanor, and it was too late now. Haltingly she explained about the betrothal contract. ''So you see why I had to come in Eleanor's place,'' she finished.

Isola looked grim. ''I remember giving August a piece of my mind when he arranged the ceremony, but he had his own ideas. I don't approve of children being promised in marriage, and your dilemma proves I'm right. Telling Prince Michel the truth is out of the question, I imagine?''

Caroline flinched at Isola's acerbic tone. ''Eleanor is afraid he'll come looking for her and put an end to any chance of her marrying Danny O'Hare-Smith.''

''It explains Eleanor's motivation but not why *you* agreed to go along.''

Caroline felt her eyebrows lift. ''I wanted to help.''

''Not yourself?''

''I don't understand. How can it help me?''

Isola's eyes bored into her. ''You're not the slightest bit in love with Prince Michel?''

''Of course not.''

Isola's hand reached for hers across the table. ''You may

be grown up, but I can still tell when you're being less than honest."

"With you?"

"With yourself. It's the real reason you agreed to the deception, isn't it?"

How could Caroline argue when she wasn't sure of the answer herself? She settled for, "I wanted to help Eleanor, but I also wanted to see Michel again."

"Then what's the problem?"

Caroline felt bleakness invade her expression. "The betrothal suits Michel because he doesn't want to marry for love." She suspected he was still loyal to the memory of Luc's mother, but she didn't say so, not sure how much of that relationship was common knowledge.

Isola looked thoughtful. "I see. And what do you want?"

"Me?" It was as if Isola's question forced her to ask it of herself for the first time. "I want...." She let her voice trail away. Not even to herself would she admit that she wanted Michel. Even if it was true, he didn't want her love. He wanted a neat arrangement that left him free to continue being the playboy prince. "What does it matter?" she went on. "When he finds out I've deceived him, he won't want anything more to do with me."

"Then as I see it, you've got nothing to lose by telling the prince the truth."

Caroline managed a wan smile. "You're right and I will, as soon as I know Eleanor is safely married to Danny."

Isola's fingers drew patterns on the monogrammed cloth. "When does the wedding take place?"

"Soon, I hope." At Isola's raised-eyebrow look, she added, "Eleanor is on a modeling assignment in Las Vegas and until she calls me, I have no way to get in touch with her."

"It's a pretty problem," Isola agreed. "Unless Eleanor

has changed greatly, she won't be in any hurry to let you off the hook.''

How well Isola knew her twin, Caroline thought. She had reached much the same conclusion but hadn't wanted to admit to herself that it was true. Now she had to face facts. She was on her own for the time being. ''Now you know the truth, what will you do?'' she asked Isola.

Her old teacher looked thoughtful. ''Exactly what Prince Michel has asked me to do—tutor you in Carramer language and customs.''

''You mean you won't betray me?''

Isola frowned. ''I won't lie to him if he asks me, and I won't call you Eleanor in his hearing. But it's not my place to point out the error of His Royal Highness's ways.''

Caroline wanted to hug her. ''It's more than I dared ask of you, Vava Rose. Thank you.''

The respectful title made Isola's eyes mist. ''You didn't ask me, I volunteered, *ma amounou*. Pity help me, I've had a soft spot for you ever since you presented me with that garland of fire flowers when you were ten.''

Caroline felt herself flush. ''I had no idea that fire flowers are traditionally presented to a virgin after her first night with a man.''

''If I'd thought you did, I would have strangled you with it,'' Isola said with a laugh. ''You weren't to know that in Carramer everything in nature has a special significance. Other countries limit themselves to a language of flowers. As well, we have a language of shells, coral, sand patterns, the fallen branches of trees, clouds, rainbows and, of course, the Mayati. At times words are almost superfluous.''

On impulse Caroline got up and went to Isola, enveloping her in a hug, a demonstration of how little she needed words to show how much she cared for her former teacher. ''I'm sorry things didn't work out with you and Dad.''

"You might have changed your mind after having me as a mother for a while," Isola said sharply.

Caroline wasn't fooled. "I don't believe it. You would have been good for all of us."

Isola wasn't given to emotional outbursts, but one hovered on her face now until she controlled it with an obvious effort. "Now say that to me again in Carramer. Formal and informal modes please, *ma amounou*."

When had his life become so complicated? Michel wondered as he strode swiftly down the corridor leading to the nursery. By degrees his confidence in a marriage based on the old betrothal contract was being eroded.

His response to his fiancée was part of the problem, he accepted. His plan didn't include falling in love and he recognized the danger he was in. He had expected her to be beautiful, even sexy. What he hadn't expected was a sweet, loving nature that spoke to needs he didn't want to admit to owning. She was either a changeling or a witch, he decided. Either way, something was amiss here, and given time he would find out what, he resolved.

Wariness mixed with pleasure as he thought of her reaction to his surprise. He had engaged Isola because he remembered the twins' fondness for their former teacher and the response hadn't disappointed him.

He clenched and unclenched his hands. She knew he expected Isola to watch her as well as tutor her, but her unrestrained joy over the reunion filled him with misgivings. In forcing her to stay, was he doing the right thing? The way she affected him tempted him to give in and let her decide whether to stay or not.

It was the "or not" that did it. Denial came as swiftly as a blow. He wasn't prepared to risk it. Witch or changeling, she belonged with him. She hadn't fully accepted it yet, but she would, in time. Appointing Isola as her watchdog ensured she would take the time.

Before his higher self pointed out the rationalization for what it was, he pushed open the nursery door. Shona sat in an antique rocking chair with Luc in her arms, the baby sucking hungrily on a bottle. The sight threatened to puncture Michel's remaining defenses.

A sudden, powerful image of a wife and their suckling baby made him blink to restore Shona's image in place of the one invading his thoughts. The vision cleared but an ache inside him remained. What was wrong with him? For a moment he had wanted the image to be real. He had wanted the love the image represented.

He was a fool. Hadn't he learned anything from his brother's experience? Love was a trap, the penalty for making a mistake a life sentence. Far better to agree to marry without love from the start, then nobody got hurt when times and needs inevitably changed.

He took the baby from Shona, supporting Luc expertly along his bent arm while the baby finished the bottle. Afterward Shona draped a towel over Michel's shoulder and he held the baby against it, taking comfort in the softness and warmth of his son's body. He stood up and started to pace as he gently rubbed the baby's back. Luc's needs were so simple and easily satisfied. Michel wished he could say the same about himself.

Chapter Six

The telephone roused Caroline as she was drifting off to sleep. She groped for the bedside light, then picked up the receiver. At the sound of her twin's voice, she jolted upright in bed. "Eleanor, where are you?"

"After I finished the assignment, Danny and I went to a hotel near the Grand Canyon. We didn't get home until this morning when I found your messages on the machine. You knew we planned to take a vacation."

Just as well she hadn't started calling hotels in Las Vegas, Caroline thought. Her twin's defensive tone wasn't lost on her. "I know and I'm not criticizing, but we need to talk. Has Danny proposed yet?"

"You make it sound so unromantic," Eleanor said, a pout in her voice. "He proposed to me by moonlight on the edge of the Grand Canyon. He'd brought champagne and glasses and we drank a toast to our future, then we went back to the hotel and danced for hours. It was the most wonderful night of my life. I'm wearing his ring right now. I wish you could see the size of the diamond."

Caroline pictured her twin holding out her left hand, the better to admire the engagement ring. Something very like jealousy gripped her, but she pushed it away. "I'm happy for both of you. I'll be happier still if you can arrange to get married right away."

A moment of stunned silence followed, then Eleanor said, "There's no rush. I'm not pregnant, after all."

Had she thought she might be? It was Caroline's turn to be left speechless. She had never guessed. No wonder Eleanor had been so panic-stricken when she thought Michel might jeopardize her relationship with Danny. "Oh, Eleanor, you should have told me," she said on a strained note. "You didn't have to deal with such a worry alone."

"All's well that ends well," Eleanor quoted, but her voice shook. "Even Danny's mother is starting to come around. When he called her yesterday with our news, she asked him to put me on and she actually welcomed me into the family." Her voice broke. "It's going to be all right, Caroline, I know it is. I love Danny so much."

"Of course it's going to be all right." Despite being the younger by a few minutes, Caroline automatically fell into the parental role she'd filled all their lives. "But you must listen to me. Prince Michel still thinks I'm you and he doesn't intend to let me leave Carramer until we're married."

"He can't do that."

"You're forgetting how much power the royal family holds in this country. He can do anything he wants."

"But you're an American citizen."

Caroline swallowed. "Maybe, but while they think I'm legally betrothed to a Carramer national and living in their country, local laws take precedence."

Eleanor's breathing sharpened as she absorbed the import of this. "I see."

"So you see why you and Danny must marry sooner rather than later? It's the only way to put you safely out of reach of Carramer law."

"I see that *you* want me married and out of the way."

Caroline recoiled physically from the anger she heard in her twin's voice. "What are you saying?"

"You can't wait to get me married and out of your hair, can you?"

Hurt beyond words, Caroline clutched the phone so hard her knuckles whitened. "That's crazy and you know it."

"Is it, Caroline? You elected yourself our mother years ago and you've given me advice and suggestions for years, whether I wanted them or not. Well, not this time. Danny's mother has finally started to warm to me. If we run off and elope now, I'll blow it big-time. She'll never speak to me again."

Caroline reeled from an image of herself as an interfering mother-substitute. It wasn't true, was it? She had imagined she was merely looking out for her twin when they had no one else, and it shocked Caroline to hear her concern being so misinterpreted.

"I'm sorry I seem as if I'm interfering," she said quietly.

"No, I'm the one who's sorry," Eleanor said quickly, remorse weighting her tone. "I shouldn't have said you act like my mother. I know you only want what's best for me. But this time what's best is for me to marry Danny in the traditional way. I want to walk down a real aisle dressed in yards and yards of white silk and have a proper wedding, not a cloak-and-dagger affair, and not wearing feathers and beads in some kooky jungle ritual."

Picturing their father's likely preference, Caroline smiled around the ache inside her. "We're both entitled, goodness knows. We put up with enough weird stuff when we were growing up. It isn't a crime to want to be normal."

"Thanks for understanding." Eleanor's gratitude sounded heartfelt. "I really am sorry I said those stupid things about you. They're not true."

"Maybe they're truer than either of us likes to think," Caroline admitted. "I do mother you sometimes and I'll try not to, although it may take a while. Habits die hard, you know."

"And I'll try to act more grown-up so you don't feel any need to mother me," Eleanor agreed. "This could be good for both of us."

Caroline laughed although her eyes felt misty. "Especially when you're a married woman with a couple of children clinging to your skirts."

"Then you can mother them instead of me. Or godmother them, if it's okay with you?"

"I'd like nothing better." Unless it was having Eleanor become godmother to *her* children came the unbidden thought. Reality rushed back to cancel the beautiful fantasy. "It doesn't solve the problem of the betrothal contract."

"No, it doesn't. There's only one solution."

If Eleanor was not to get married right away, Caroline couldn't think what else would put her beyond Michel's reach. When she said so, her twin sounded frustrated. "The problem isn't keeping me away from Michel, it's getting you out of Carramer. We can worry about the rest later."

Caroline was about to say that *later* had a way of catching up, but bit back the comment. She was out of the mothering business as of now. "What do you have in mind?" she asked.

"I take it you can't simply board a plane and fly home?"

Caroline shook her head, then realized that Eleanor couldn't see the gesture. "The prince has someone watching me all the time. He hasn't said so, but I'm sure they're under orders to prevent me from leaving."

"Caroline Temple isn't betrothed to Michel. If you tell him who you are, he'll have no excuse to detain you." Eleanor sensed Caroline's hesitation. "You care about him, don't you? Is that why you don't want to confess?"

Caroline was no closer to answering the question now than when Isola Rose had asked it earlier. "Confessing won't stop Michel from enforcing the contract," she dissembled.

"He'd have to kidnap me to get me away from Danny." After a shocked pause, she added, "You don't think he'd go that far, do you?"

"I hope not. He's used to people obeying his every command, but even royalty can't flout international law."

"I don't think I want to find out the hard way, so telling him the truth is out. Better to let him think I was there and got away."

Easy for Eleanor to say, Caroline thought. Her twin anticipated her objection. "Since you can't leave by regular means, we'll have to be devious. Among the mail waiting for me when I got back was a postcard from that couple we met in Australia. Do you remember Dr. Walter Sloane and his wife, Mildred?"

Caroline wondered what they had to do with the problem at hand. "The American marine biologists? Of course I do, but what—"

"According to their card, they're still living and working aboard their cruiser."

"The *Sargasso*," Caroline remembered, still puzzled. The twins and their father had accompanied the couple on an expedition from Darwin to Cape York and Thursday Island. It had been one of the highlights of her young existence.

"That's the one. Well, guess what? Right now, *Sargasso*

is moored not half a mile from you at the underwater observatory on Isle des Anges.''

"I still don't see…oh.''

"Yes, oh. I'm sure if you ask the Sloanes, they will let you go with them when they leave.''

Caroline chewed her lower lip. "They must be here under Michel's patronage. I don't want to get them into trouble with him.''

"You won't. According to Mildred, they're about to head back to the States and retire to a research center they've set up in Florida. It doesn't sound as if they're returning to Carramer anytime soon.''

"I still don't like the idea of involving anyone else.''

"Any more than you like the idea of leaving Michel, admit it,'' Eleanor said with a sigh of exasperation. "Why couldn't Dad have promised you to him instead of me? Then it wouldn't be a problem.''

Eleanor wasn't allowing for Michel's desire to retain his freedom within marriage, Caroline thought. Having a wife who actually cared for him wasn't part of his plans. She said as much to Eleanor, adding, "I think he's still in love with the mother of his child.''

There was a gasp from Eleanor. "He has a *child?*''

Caroline had forgotten that her sister didn't know. "He has an adorable nine-month-old baby called Luc whose mother died soon after he was born. Michel is raising him alone. I gather there was a fuss in the media here when he acknowledged the baby as his son, but he did it anyway. I suspect that part of the prince's heart died with Luc's mother.''

Eleanor whistled softly. "It would explain why Michel is so determined to hold you—that is me—to that damned contract. Where else would he find the wife protocol expects of him, who'll also be a mother to his son without demanding too much in return?''

''It isn't as heartless as you make it sound.''

''Then tell me what his wife is supposed to get out of the arrangement?''

There was no avoiding an answer. ''The sort of marriage you said in print that you wanted.''

''Are you saying *I* gave Michel the idea to enforce the contract?''

''Since it suits him as well, he can't see why I—that is, you—have a problem.''

''But you can. When I said in print that a rich husband meant more to me than love and romance, I hadn't met Danny. I didn't know how it felt to love someone to the depths of your being. If Danny didn't have a cent to his name, I'd still want to spend the rest of my life with him.''

Caroline believed her, but it didn't solve their predicament. ''It's starting to look as if the Sloanes are the only way out.''

''Then you'll ask them to help you?''

''As soon as I work out how to get in touch with them without arousing Michel's suspicion.''

A restless night left her no closer to a solution, and the next morning Michel was hurrying off to an official engagement, leaving them no time to talk. On his way out he said she would accompany him next time. Although she murmured agreement, the idea appalled her. She couldn't keep appearing at his side as his bride-to-be, knowing she was a total fraud.

She didn't begrudge Eleanor her happiness with Danny, but she wished it hadn't left her feeling so alone. Facing the future without her twin was going to be much harder than she had expected even without the present dilemma.

Need clawed at her, as fierce as it was unexpected. She wanted to be cherished the way Danny cherished Eleanor. To be loved. By Michel? She shook her head, furious with her own thoughts. It wasn't going to happen and she might as well accept it. The prince wanted a wife and the heirs his position required, but without strings.

He must have loved Luc's mother a great deal if losing her had soured him on marriage for good, she thought. Deceiving him was hardly likely to improve his opinion.

She was glad to have a lesson with Isola to distract herself from such unproductive thoughts. If Isola found Caroline unusually keen to throw herself into her studies, she didn't say so, and the time passed quickly.

"Can you stay for lunch?" she asked when Isola declared the lesson over.

Isola rubbed her jaw and said in Carramer, "I can't. I have a dentist's appointment."

Caroline smiled in sympathy, saying in the same language, "Would you like some company?"

Isola shook her head and switched to English. "Thanks for the offer, but my sister already volunteered to come with me. And speaking of sisters…"

"I spoke to Eleanor. She's afraid that if she elopes with Danny, her prospective mother-in-law may never speak to her again."

Isola covered Caroline's hand with her own in silent sympathy. "So she isn't coming. What will you do now?"

"Think of another solution." Unwilling to involve Isola any more deeply, Caroline held back from mentioning the Sloanes and their cruiser.

"Wouldn't telling the truth be simpler?"

Simpler but not wise, while Eleanor was unmarried and therefore still vulnerable. Caroline shook her head. "There's nothing simple about this situation."

"Not if your feelings for Prince Michel keep getting in the way."

"I don't have feelings for him," she denied. How many times did she have to say it to how many people before they believed it?

Before she believed it herself?

The teacher's level gaze met Caroline's. "You forget how well I know you. You may be grown up, but you still look away when you're being less than honest with me."

"Is that how you could always tell me when we were up to something?"

"That and a teacher's instincts. Right now, they tell me you have strong feelings for our prince, but you're reluctant to admit them. Why?"

"He doesn't want them."

"What makes you so certain he doesn't."

Caroline felt her shoulders droop as she explained about Michel's views on marriage, her voice becoming hesitant when she got to the part about Luc's mother.

Isola nodded. "I had heard the rumors that Luc is his love child, although I'm not sure I believe them."

Caroline was intrigued. "Why not?"

"The Prince Michel I know is far less of a womanizer than he likes us to think. Making it look as if he plays the field may be his way of fending off unwanted marriage overtures. He is also extraordinarily compassionate. How better to protect and provide for an orphaned baby than to encourage the belief that Luc is his own offspring?"

It was a possibility Caroline hadn't considered and it certainly showed Michel in a different light. Michel had said that Luc was his son, but it could mean by adoption. How would she feel about him then? She sighed. Her own behavior made the question academic.

Isola misinterpreted her pupil's sigh. "Even if Michel

was in love with Luc's mother, it doesn't mean he can never love again, but it may take time.''

Caroline squeezed her tutor's arm. "Thanks, Vava Rose. I appreciate your advice.''

Isola made a face and said in Carramer, "Advice is easy. Acting on it is the hard part.''

After farewelling her in the same language, Caroline slumped onto an antique chaise. Part of her was more than ready to believe Isola. If Michel had adopted Luc out of the goodness of his heart, it changed everything. But it didn't change the fact that Caroline had set out to deceive him. Any man would have trouble with that, and Michel wasn't just any man.

She recalled her own fury at being deceived by Ralph. It seemed so long ago now, but her feelings of betrayal lingered, though they'd dimmed with time. Michel would be entitled to his anger, although she quailed at the thought of being on the receiving end. She had only seen him truly furious once years ago, when he caught a gardener harassing a young housemaid. Only a teenager himself, Michel had cowed the man with a tirade worthy of the monarch himself, reducing the evildoer to a stuttering mess.

A shiver shook her as she imagined Michel's wrath directed at her. When had his good opinion become so all-important? It had always been important, she thought on a heavy outrush of breath. When they were younger, a word of praise from him had been worth any amount of compliments from someone else. She still hungered for it and knew it had a lot to do with why she put off telling him the truth. Having him regard her with loathing would feel like having her heart ripped out.

Driven to action, she wandered until she came to a conservatory that Michel had pointed out to her soon after her arrival. It was one of several serving the palace. Here, flowers were kept fresh until they were arranged for display in the palace.

It was lunchtime so the conservatory was deserted. Caroline slipped inside and the glass door whispered shut behind her. Great containers of gladiolus, long-stemmed roses, orchids, ferns and a dozen other tropical blooms stood in containers of water awaiting attention. She filled her lungs with the perfumed air.

Before she had the thought fully hatched, she had moved to a table and pulled a crystal vase toward her. With the ease of long practice, she selected, trimmed and arranged several sprays of ginger orchids amid cloud-soft silver fern fronds. The work felt good. She hummed to herself as the arrangement took shape.

She hadn't realized how much she missed being around growing things, she thought as her fingers flew. Perspiration dewed her skin from the humidity in the room and one fingernail had splintered, but she felt happy for the first time in days.

"You have a smudge on your forehead."

Startled out of her absorption, she whirled around to find Michel watching her from the doorway. Her breath caught. He looked magnificent in his ceremonial uniform. The dress whites emphasized the healthy glow of his skin and made his dark gaze seem more intense than usual.

The epaulets made his shoulders look sinfully broad, but it was nothing compared to what the lean cut of the uniform pants did for the rest of his shape. She felt her knees weaken. He had no right to look so devastatingly appealing when she was a damp mess.

She scrubbed at the offending smudge. "Gone now?"

"Permit me."

Removing a spotless white handkerchief from his pocket he dipped it into a font of springwater and dabbed at her forehead. The icy water should have chilled her, but instead she felt her skin catch fire.

"Better?" Strange how hard it was to force words out around her suddenly parched throat.

"Much better."

He was so close the scent of him filled her nostrils. Traces of his aftershave lotion made her think of rivers and woodlands, wild places where they could be alone. She dragged in a breath. "Thank you."

"You're welcome." He didn't move away but dropped his hands to her shoulders as if to pull her closer. "When I found you here, you looked so at home that I had to blink to assure myself that it was really you."

The enormity of her mistake washed over her. To Eleanor, a greenhouse should hold as much appeal as a catwalk would to Caroline. She hadn't thought. With her mind in turmoil she had naturally gravitated to the one place she felt at ease. "How long have you been watching me?"

Long enough to wish she'd look at him with the same preoccupation that she did the flowers, Michel thought. Jealousy gripped him along with an irrational inclination to hurl the orchids across the room. He would feel the same about anything that competed with himself for her attention, he thought in some astonishment.

Aloud he said, "Long enough. You looked so happy I didn't have the heart to disturb you."

Her breath tightened in her throat. "I needed something to occupy myself," she explained.

"If all you need is occupying..." He finished the thought by moving his mouth closer and touching his lips to hers.

The conservatory spun and she pressed her hands against his chest to steady herself. The rock-solid feel of him had the opposite effect, causing the world to shift under her feet.

Feeling her sway, he gathered her against him and found

her mouth again, this time with a need he hadn't admitted even to himself until he gave in to it. Her mouth felt warm and pliant, her breath tasting sweet and minty when she opened her lips in response to the pressure he exerted.

Emboldened by her lack of resistance, he teased her tongue with his in a sinuous dance that speared him with desire to the very depths of his being. He knew she felt it, too, because her hands cupped his neck, drawing him closer, drinking him in with as much urgency as he was tasting her.

Michel fought himself. Where was the playboy prince now? He had taken what he wanted, given pleasure as skillfully as he knew how, but never let any woman control him beyond the moment. Yet this morning he had met with various high-ranking officers and launched a new naval vessel, aware of performing his duties like a man in a dream.

He felt his defenses crumbling and knew he should stop this before she touched the core of his being, found the small boy he nurtured there as every man did, protected from the world and from hurt. Found *him*. He should but he didn't. He went on kissing her as if his life depended on it. One some level, he suspected it did.

Once in his life he had experienced a mild case of nitrogen narcosis from scuba diving too deeply. Holding her in his arms, he felt the same dangerous euphoria start to build. Pain and pleasure warred inside him. He wanted her. He needed her.

He didn't need the vulnerability that she represented.

Even so, it took everything he had to draw away from her, and still he kept his arms around her while his breath mingled with hers. He found the spot on her forehead where he'd removed the smudge and lightly touched his lips to it. It was enough to make her gasp. He knew why. His whole body throbbed with heat and need. Much more of this and he would take her here and now, and to perdition with who might stumble on them.

Until his baby son came into his life, no breath of scandal had been allowed to touch the royal house. Yet here he was contemplating making love in a conservatory.

Anger replaced passion and he was finally able to draw away from her. He had never allowed any woman such power over him. What was he doing allowing it now with the one woman he should keep at arm's length?

When he stepped away, Caroline looked as if her legs would buckle. Blindly she clutched at the table behind her. It took everything Michel had not to pull her back into his arms and support her with his strength. It wouldn't end with support, he knew, well aware of where it would end. And how inappropriate it would be.

For possibly the first time in his life he was tempted to let propriety go hang. But he was royal enough not to and he saw her read the decision in his eyes.

She knew she looked as crushed as she felt. She should have appreciated his strength. Lord knew, it was more than she had been able to call on. Instead she felt bereft, wanting him to use his strength for quite another purpose, to surround her and fill her until she was mindless with sensual pleasure.

Shock coiled through her. Where was the prim, proper Caroline Temple now? She who was so proud of saving herself for a love beyond all others. Living as Eleanor must be affecting her in ways she hadn't anticipated. This had to end before she lost herself entirely in the face of Michel's powerful allure.

The Sloanes. Like a lifeline, she clung to the name and the possibility of escape. It had suddenly become more urgent than ever. She faced facts. She needed to get away as much for her own survival as to protect Eleanor.

She saw Michel watching her, his expression thoughtful. "I suggest that we make the wedding soon."

She turned her anger at herself against him, although there was little enough satisfaction in it. "Because you can't control yourself?"

"I believe I just did. But I'm not made of iron and neither, it is obvious, are you, my beautiful siren."

"If you think I enjoyed that—"

"I don't think it, I know it. Another second or two in my arms and you'd have gone up in flames."

Her face betrayed her, she knew. Clenching her fists, she tried another approach. "I told you this marriage isn't a good idea."

One dark eyebrow tilted quizzically. "I'd say we just demonstrated why it's a superbly good idea."

"Sex isn't everything," she snapped, angry at being read so accurately. "You admit you don't want to marry for love. What if I've decided that I do?"

He angled his body against the door frame and crossed his arms over his broad chest. "This is rather a switch for you, isn't it?"

"People change," she pointed out.

He nodded. "Even so, it's quite a leap from gold-digging adventuress to loving wife."

She bridled at hearing Eleanor described so unflatteringly. "Do you have to put it so bluntly?"

He ticked points off on his fingers. "In the interview, you mentioned the duke's son, then the fashion designer, the newspaper magnate—twenty years older than you, but generous to a fault. You dumped him for—"

"All right, I get the picture," she snapped, wishing fervently that Eleanor had been more discreet.

"Are you saying you weren't reported accurately?" he asked reasonably.

Her heart sank. The article was accurate, unfortunately. Eleanor had never claimed to be a one-man woman, only one man at a time. She had also rejected men Caroline considered to be far nicer, merely because they weren't rich. "No," she said in a low voice.

"Am I not rich enough for you? Isn't the title of princess to your liking?"

"This has nothing to do with money or titles."

"Then what?"

"Love," she admitted softly. "Is wanting to be loved so unreasonable?"

The silence spun out until it was almost tangible. Her breathing sounded loud in her ears, and she felt her control slipping again. Another second and she would go to him, link her arms around his neck and offer her mouth for his kiss, not caring where or if it would end. She wanted him that much.

He lifted his shoulders, then let them drop as his taut gaze bored into her. "I can promise you won't want for love. I shall pay homage to you in the most sacred way, by worshipping at the temple of your body as frequently as we both desire. As my consort, you'll have my name, children, lands, titles and the wealth of the kingdom to show the world how greatly you are loved. I can offer you no more."

Caroline's mouth dried. She had a sudden, vivid image of herself in his bed. She had already enjoyed a taste of his skill as a lover and to think it could be just the beginning.... The temptation was almost too great. It took an effort of will to shake her head. "You still don't understand. Apart from children, the rest are only *things*. They're no substitute for a good relationship."

"Can you really have changed so much?"

She spread her hands wide in a gesture of surrender.

"Perhaps not as much as you think. But doesn't it prove that a marriage between us is a terrible idea?"

"I perceive that you want me to think it is for some purpose of your own," he drawled, sounding suddenly dangerous.

Her senses went on alert. "What do you mean?"

"I should have seen it before. Your sudden insistence on the importance of love is a ploy, isn't it?"

"What are you talking about?"

He gave a humorless laugh. "Perhaps wealth and titles aren't sufficiently challenging anymore. Is this the ultimate challenge, to bring me to my knees before you?"

She felt her face drain of color. "I would never—"

"Save it." His tone of royal command sliced through her denial. "I understand you perhaps better than you do yourself. Making men want you is quite a game, isn't it? You can't bear the thought of being unable to control me, so you've decided to try something new—make me fall in love with you. What happens if I do?"

She remained stubbornly mute. This was his script. She wanted no part of it.

"I suppose you'd enjoy throwing my love right back in my face," he concluded.

Unwillingly she heard the bitter experience in his voice and wondered at its source. Perhaps Isola was wrong. Losing Luc's mother might have hurt him so badly that he was not prepared to risk having it happen again.

"Shall I read your silence as agreement?" he asked.

She shook off the concern. "Read it as you will. You have the upper hand, Your Highness." *For now,* she added to herself.

He looked mildly surprised. "Such ready agreement? I thought I might have to convince you."

His gaze settling on her mouth told her how he would

have set about it. A lump filled her throat, but she refused to swallow and let him see how deeply he affected her. For a moment she was tempted to offer another argument solely so he would make good his threat.

As if sensing her temptation, he moved closer. Her pulse went haywire. But he merely ran the pad of his thumb across her lower lip in a tantalizing imitation of a kiss. The supposedly innocent gesture filled her with desires that were anything but innocent. When he let his hand drop to his side, she wanted to weep with frustration.

"Soon," he said, although she hadn't asked a question. "Your silence is for the best, for now. It will be far more…stimulating…arguing the shape of our relationship in our marriage bed. However, my endurance is not limitless, so I will announce our wedding date within the week."

Chapter Seven

She fought to keep the alarm off her face. She couldn't let Michel announce their wedding date so soon. It gave her precious little time to meet the Sloanes and enlist their help in getting away from Carramer.

They could refuse, but she wouldn't think of that now. They had to help her. This couldn't go on any longer. Deceiving Michel and his staff was bad enough. The attention showered on her by the royal household and the Aquarium staff warned her what to expect from the people of Carramer after she was officially proclaimed as their future princess. She couldn't allow it to happen.

Caroline felt like a passenger on a runaway roller coaster. How had things gotten so far out of hand.

Not things, her feelings toward Michel, she thought ruefully. If she hadn't let him kiss her so passionately, he wouldn't have felt driven to announce a wedding date.

Let him? She almost laughed aloud. She had practically begged him, returning his kisses with mortifying abandon. But for his strength they would be making love among the flowers at this moment. Barely capable of standing under her own power, her whole body shaking with the force of her arousal, she couldn't have stopped him to save her life. She hadn't wanted to stop him, she acknowledged. She wanted the sweet torment to go on to its ultimate conclusion.

She should hate him for dismissing her wish to marry for love as a trick. Had she really been Eleanor, his suspicion might once have been justified. Caroline was the one yearning for the once-and-forever love the books wrote about and the songs sang about. To her, true love went far beyond mutual desire. In this she and Michel were as compatible as a snowman and a Carramer beach.

Michel hooked a finger inside his uniform collar. It felt tight suddenly, although it had fitted perfectly until he walked into the conservatory. He hadn't planned to impose a wedding date so soon. But wanting her as much as he did, it had better be sooner rather than later or he wouldn't answer for the consequences.

She looked stunned. "Can you think of any reason to delay?" he asked. "It's obvious we both know what we want."

"You're wrong about what I want," she said, sounding shaky. She played with the flowers as if she needed something to occupy her hands. Watching her slide the thick stem of a trumpet lily between her fingers, he felt as if he would explode.

Desire stabbed through him making his blood sing and his eyes burn. He wanted to take her here and now, without ceremony, driving out all doubts once and for all. She already belonged to him. Why not take what was his by right?

But he couldn't. For perhaps the first time he held back, the vulnerability he saw in her eyes undermining his certainty. He had never taken any woman by force, never needed to. He doubted whether force would be needed now. Still, her look of fragility stopped him.

"Do you deny wanting me?" he asked.

Her head came up. He was grimly pleased when she didn't take refuge in a lie. "No."

He heard the cost of her confession in the one whispered word. Something twisted inside him, overriding his body's demands with the desire to protect—his mate? The feeling was at once ancient and compellingly new, at odds with his plan for a no-strings marriage. What was going on?

Angry with himself, he withdrew behind his royal mask. Lord knew, he'd had plenty of practice at it, although never for this reason. "Then the marriage will take place as soon as possible."

"The marriage, Michel? You make it sound cold and forbidding, like a business transaction."

"What else would you call it?"

Aware that she was speaking for herself more than for Eleanor, Caroline said, "A little romance wouldn't hurt."

Her wistful tone caught him off-guard, threatening to crack the royal mask. "I remind you that this marriage is for mutual benefit, not romance."

"Your benefit," she corrected, becoming angry. He winced as her fingers clenched around the lily stem until he expected to hear it snap. "You gain a consort, a bedmate and a mother for your children without sacrificing any of your personal freedom. What does your wife get?"

He felt his mouth soften into a smile. He couldn't help himself. "I should have thought you'd know the answer by now."

Since she obviously didn't, he felt duty-bound to give her another demonstration. The aching need to hold her in his arms again had nothing to do with it, he told himself. Before she could muster her defense he lifted the hapless lily out of her hands and set it aside, then stepped into the space between them and skimmed his lips over the side of her neck.

Her reaction was instantaneous. Her hands slid around his back, the splayed fingers fiery through his uniform and she pulled him close, turning her face up to his, her lips slightly parted.

It was all the invitation he needed and more than he had hoped for. When he nuzzled her lips farther apart and ran his tongue along her lower lip, she gasped but didn't attempt to shut him out. She was getting the hang of this, he thought in some surprise, as he heard her moan softly, deep in her throat. He had intended to show her what she could expect from their marriage. Now he started to wonder who was teaching whom.

Her scent surrounded him, light as a butterfly, potent as a field of flowers, making him feel light-headed and off-center, as if he had been standing too long in the midday sun. His hands tightened on her shoulders as he resisted the feeling. No part of his plan involved surrendering to a woman's power, especially not this woman.

She turned her head slightly so their lips were no longer aligned. "It won't work," she said on a heavy sigh.

He nibbled the soft pad of her earlobe. "I thought it was working perfectly."

"For you, maybe." The denial sounded forced when accompanied by her sharp intake of breath. Encouraged, he nibbled again.

"Will you stop that?"

Her eyes blazed as she wrenched herself away from him and stood braced with her back against the table, her fingers curling around the edge as if she would like to pick it up and hurl it at him. Her chest moved up and down in time with her labored breathing, and there was a definite flush to her cheeks. "I can't think straight when you do that."

"That was the general idea," he said, annoyed to find that he didn't feel much calmer. He felt overheated and his heart thudded uncomfortably.

She threw him a mutinous look. "I'm not some wild creature that you can use seduction to tame."

He answered with a level look of his own. "Wild is moot. In any case it seems to have the opposite effect. Not that I'm complaining." For all the fireworks, she didn't sound all that unhappy, either. She sounded more…alarmed…at her own responses, as if he had touched some part of her that she usually kept off-limits.

Damned if he didn't feel something similar.

Impossible, he told himself. He didn't love women, he made love to them. Keeping part of himself aloof was his insurance against getting too involved. He had no intention of changing even for his wife. Especially for his wife.

But he couldn't stop thinking of how she felt in his arms. How she tasted and smelled. How she moved. Angry, she was magnificent. Aroused, she was exciting. He wanted to see her drugged with passion, wanting him so much that she couldn't think straight. Then he wanted to take her flying. Their feet were already barely on the ground. Thinking of how much higher they could go together ignited his body like a furnace and the blood sang in his ears.

The one thing he had always avoided was love, and it frustrated him that it was all she seemed to want. Didn't she sense how much more they could share? What difference could a few little words make?

"Would it help if I say I love you?" he asked, testing the water. He had never said anything remotely like it to any woman, but it came out astonishingly easily.

She grabbed the lily and flung it at him. It impacted soggily against his chest and dropped to the floor, leaving a green smear on his dress uniform. She went white and clutched a hand to her mouth. "I'm sorry, I didn't mean to do that."

Well, he had his answer, he thought soberly. "It will clean, but I'll hear about it from my valet," he said dryly. "Luckily, throwing flowers at a member of the royal family isn't a criminal act."

She picked up his discarded handkerchief, dipped it in water and scrubbed at the stain. "All the same, it was childish and I apologize."

Childish wasn't how he would describe her behavior, he thought. The attempted cleanup brought her uncomfortably close again, putting all sorts of very adult ideas in his head. This would have to stop. With an effort he slowed his breathing and caught her wrists, holding her away from him. "I said it will clean."

She looked at the hands locked around her wrists and he saw her breathing constrict. In an unsteady voice, she said, "In that case, may I go now? I haven't had lunch yet."

He released her with a reluctance that was better not examined too closely. "Neither have I. I planned to take Luc for a picnic down at the marina. Would you like to join us?"

She shook her head. "The two of you need to spend time together. I'll only be in the way."

He lifted his hands, palms upward, reading the reluctance she tried to hide from him. "If you prefer, I can bring Shona along as chaperone," he offered.

He had no intention of taking the nanny with them and was relived when she smiled hesitantly. "Do we need a chaperone?"

"Come with us and see for yourself."

He watched her war with herself. He could order her

along, but he balked at it for some reason. Telling himself it was a poor basis for a relationship, he knew the reason went deeper. He wanted her to come of her own accord.

Waiting for an answer was another novelty for him. He exhaled heavily as she said, "Very well. Give me time to change."

His rueful glance took in his stained uniform. "I don't plan to go like this. Meet me at the entrance to the west wing in half an hour."

She must be crazy, she told herself as she stepped out of her dress and reached for the calf-length cotton pants and halter top her maid had set out for her.

The woman would have helped her to dress, but Caroline had dismissed her, needing a few minutes alone to recover her composure. Michel had done no more than kiss her, but she felt ravaged. Clutching the clothes, she cast a wide-eyed look at herself in the mirror. Her hollow-cheeked image stared back at her above a body made leaner by the strain of pretending to be Eleanor. As a result her legs looked even more coltlike than usual and her breasts seemed fuller in contrast to her slender torso. Other than that, she looked no different. So why did she feel so changed?

In those few minutes in the conservatory she had crossed some boundary, she sensed. She had wanted Michel to make love to her more than she had ever wanted anything in her life. More, she had wanted to give *him* pleasure beyond *his* experience.

She couldn't teach him anything about lovemaking. The very idea made her want to laugh hollowly. He had already taught her more than any man she had ever known.

But she could show him the joy of sharing yourself with another person and that *was* new to him, she guessed. She had always had Eleanor as her confidant. Who had been there for Michel? His brother, Lorne, had been preoccupied with the demands of his future monarchy, and his sister, Adrienne, besides being younger, had shared few of Michel's interests.

Perhaps being royal required a certain aloofness, but in Michel, Caroline sensed a deeper aloneness that she ached to ease almost as much as she wanted to make love to him.

Definitely crazy, she told herself, frowning at her reflection. Eleanor was his fiancée, not Caroline. She had no business imagining herself as his soul mate when it was obviously the last thing he wanted. Mate, yes. But bed mate was more like it.

Cleansing anger ripped through her, replacing confusion if not desire. Take the blindfold off and face reality, she instructed herself. Treat this picnic as a test. Prove to yourself that you can be alone with him and not be turned on in the least.

Her reflection returned her dubious glance. She didn't have to be alone with him to be turned on by him. Thinking of him was more than enough.

She arrived at the west door on time, but Michel was there ahead of her with the baby in his arms. He had changed into navy shorts and a white open-necked shirt, revealing a glimpse of tanned chest that had her licking dry lips in dismay. His legs were bare and he had dark leather sandals on his feet. He looked the essence of maleness with the face and stance of a conqueror, or the unconquerable. So much for resistance, she thought, feeling what little remained to her ebbing away.

She swallowed hard. The prince and the baby made an appealing study in contrasts—soft cooing child against hard, muscular chest. Michel held the baby with confidence, not the way many men did, as if they could break the child. He looked at ease in his role as a father, making faces and funny noises in his throat until Luc laughed so delightedly that her heart almost stopped. She glanced around seeking something to carry or do to avoid facing the tableau that needed only a mother figure to complete it.

"Everything we need is in the car," the prince said, anticipating her. She tried not to notice how his gaze lingered appreciatively on the slim cut of the white pants or the halter top that left her shoulders and back exposed. She was foolishly tempted to cross her arms over herself or to retreat and change into less revealing clothing.

When he said, "Ready?" she nodded, not trusting herself to speak. "Then let's go. Luc isn't the only ravenous one."

His choice of words sliced through her. Hunger described her state very well, but she doubted whether food could satisfy this appetite, if Michel had meant food at all.

Waving away the servant who rushed to help, Michel led the way to the car and strapped the baby into his car seat. She used the time to recover her composure. She was doing well until he opened the car door for her and brushed her back with his open palm as he helped her into the seat. The small touch was all it took to set every nerve on fire. Desire leaped and anger flared, at odds with each other.

When he reached for her seat belt, she seized on the anger. "I can manage, thank you." She snapped the seat belt fastened with a finality he couldn't misread.

"As you wish." There was amusement in his pewter gaze, instead of the rejection she had intended to put there.

"Aren't we going to the marina?" she queried tensely when he aimed the car in the opposite direction. Having Michel at the wheel when she had expected a driver to chaperone them was confusing enough, but she had nursed some thought of spotting the Sloanes' cruiser and mentioning it casually, then working the conversation around to the idea of a visit.

"I don't have time to visit the yacht today so I decided we'll picnic on the beach. Disappointed?" he asked as he controlled the powerful car with easy movements.

Not as much as she probably should be, she thought. Aloud, she said, "The beach is fine. I brought a hat and sun lotion."

"There's more in the basket," he said. "Along with everything else. The kitchen packed enough food to feed an army."

He hesitated then said, "You're angry."

She avoided looking at him. "Observant of you."

"Because I kissed you?"

Because she had enjoyed it more than she had any business doing. "Of course not," she snapped, then forced herself to respond as Eleanor. "It's not as if it was the first time."

"Hardly." The single word held anger and something else—disappointment? She had invited it but didn't care for how much it hurt. In spite of what he thought, no man had kissed her the way he did, transporting her to realms of pleasure she had only imagined until now. Nor had she wanted to give herself to a man so much that it was killing her not to surrender to it—and him—completely.

Before she did anything stupid like admitting it, she took a deep breath. "I was hoping to catch up with some people whose boat is supposed to be moored at the marina."

He flicked her a speculative glance. "Perhaps I know them?"

"Their names are Walter and Mildred Sloane. They're marine biologists from America."

He nodded. "They're studying dolphin communication as guests of the Royal Institute for Marine Research."

"One of your projects?" she guessed.

"One of the advantages of being royal is the ability to

indulge oneself occasionally. Their research is fascinating, and I observe the project as often as my duties permit. How do you know the Sloanes?''

"Dad worked with Dr. and Mrs. Sloane in Australia," she said. "We cruised with them around the coast between Darwin and Thursday Island. Living on their boat for all those weeks, we became practically family. They're wonderful people."

"Singularly dedicated," he agreed. "Unfortunately, their work here is almost at an end."

She didn't have to pretend disappointment. "Oh, no."

"However, I have a standing invitation to dine with them aboard *Sargasso*," he went on. "I had accepted an invitation to join them for a farewell dinner before they leave for America. I'm sure they would be delighted if I bring you along."

She released a breath she had hardly been aware of holding. "That would be wonderful, thank you. How much longer will they be here?"

"Only a few more days. Dr. Sloane intends to retire to his research facility in Florida."

It tallied with what Eleanor had told her about the couple's plans. "When do you think you'll see them?" she asked, masking her impatience with an effort.

He heard it anyway. "Don't worry, I won't let them sail away until you've renewed your friendship. I'm not entirely insensitive to your feelings."

"Even though you insist on going through with this farce of a marriage?"

"It didn't feel farcical earlier," he reminded her levelly.

She could hardly argue. The reminder alone triggered such internal havoc that her composure was threatened. "Must you reduce everything to the physical?" she asked angrily, although she suspected it was as much with herself as with him.

"It seems to be the one thing we agree on," he said mildly. "You can't deny that it's a useful starting point for a marriage."

"But not the only ingredient."

He shot her a curious look. "Not if the desire is for a lifetime commitment. Then factors like communication and shared interests come into it—Shakespeare's 'marriage of true minds' if you will."

Even if he had wanted such a thing, his betrothal to Eleanor could hardly be described as a marriage of true minds. "Some people find the idea appealing," she observed.

"Unlike you and me, you mean?"

Did she imagine it or did his long fingers tighten around the steering wheel as he made the comment? It seemed unlikely. He believed her to be as open-minded about marriage as he was determined to be. Discussing it seemed futile and she couldn't change his mind about her without betraying her true identity, so she lapsed into silence.

She had achieved her aim of convincing Michel to take her with him to visit the Sloanes. She should be content. The restlessness she felt was impatience, she told herself, and reluctance to enlist her friends' help to leave Carramer. It had nothing to do with wanting to stay. That made no sense at all.

The beach was linked to the palace gardens by a private road so the drive lasted only a few minutes before Michel pulled up within sight of the rolling surf. Signs at both ends of the pristine crescent of sand proclaimed it a royal enclave. "This is your own beach?" she asked, trying to remember if she had ever come here as a child. She didn't think so.

"The land was added to the royal estate after you left,"

the prince second-guessed her. "I find it difficult to dive in peace from a public beach."

"Not to mention being surrounded by security guards," she said, looking around. A vehicle had shadowed them since leaving the palace, but the guards, if such they were, maintained a discreet distance.

He shrugged. "One learns to live with it, as you will in time."

"I don't need protection," she insisted, shuddering visibly at the thought of being watched everywhere she went.

He looked angry suddenly. "Nevertheless, you will allow the guards to do their job."

"Because you don't trust me?" she flung at him, her own anger rising.

"Because you are precious to me," he said so fiercely that she stared at him in amazement. Then she realized that her value was purely as his future consort, not for any other reason.

A knot formed in her stomach. How would it feel to be precious to him for her own sake? It felt so compelling—and so unlikely—that she felt herself pale. "Keep saying things like that and I'll start thinking you care about me," she said, unable to stop her voice from shaking.

"Shouldn't I care about you?"

She looked at him in confusion. "It isn't part of the bargain."

"Love isn't part of the bargain," he said harshly. "With no possibility of divorce, I prefer to marry for other reasons. It doesn't mean I don't care. What is love anyway?"

Depressing a control, she opened the car window and drew in sea air to the limit of her lungs and still felt short of breath. "Love is caring for another person at least as much as you care for yourself," she said.

She saw his glance dart to the car seat where the baby

gurgled happily, looking angelic with his tiny hands fisted beneath his chin. Michel's eyes gentled as he gazed at his son. "There," she said in triumph. "You feel it for Luc, don't you?"

The prince returned his gaze to her. "My son means the world to me, but he is not likely to seek another in my place."

"Is that what happened to you, Michel? Were you betrayed in love?"

His wide shoulders tensed. "It's hardly your affair."

"It is if I am to be your wife."

"There's no 'if' about it. We will be married within the month."

"Yet you wouldn't tell me why you're so cynical about love?"

He shouldered his way out of the car, came around to her side and helped her from the seat without uttering a word. By the time he had started releasing Luc from the car seat, she had had enough.

She planted a hand on his shoulder, fighting the physical sensations that shot through her the instant she made contact. "Talk to me, Michel. If we're to be man and wife, you owe me at least that much."

He spun around, his expression furious. He glared at her until she let her hand drop away. "I owe you nothing except my name and worldly goods. My thoughts and actions remain my own."

"Then so will mine. I won't marry you."

She hadn't intended to say any such thing and consternation gripped her as she realized she had all but forgotten she wasn't the one betrothed to him. She opened her mouth to retract the rash statement, but he silenced her with a gesture.

"So we get to the truth at last. Your noble protestations

about love are merely an excuse to control and manipulate the situation.''

"You'd know more about control and manipulation than I would, Your Highness." She was beyond reason now, managing to make his title come out more like an accusation.

His furious look raked her. "Explain."

"I came to Carramer freely, to discuss an old betrothal contract. Yet you knew when you sent the invitation that you didn't intend to let me leave until the contract was fulfilled. If that isn't manipulation, I don't know what is."

"This is." With the speed of a hunting predator he spun away from the baby in the capsule and planted a hand on each side of her body, effectively trapping her against the car. Before she could react, he bent his head and kissed her. There was nothing gentle or considerate about the way he plundered her mouth, and she found herself responding with an intensity that should have set every internal alarm she possessed ringing frantically. It didn't.

Her thoughts scrambled. Her pulse hammered. In that instant, nothing and no one existed for her beyond Michel. At that moment she knew that whatever he asked of her, she would give him willingly, joyfully. Surrender was so close she felt herself sway toward him.

His hands on her arms held her upright and away from him for long moments until she forced her eyes open, wondering if she looked as shocked as she felt. It was an effort to pretend indifference, and she suspected she failed as she demanded, "Are you quite through?"

"For now, since my point is made. If I really set out to manipulate you, you would stand no chance of resistance. So your talk of being manipulated over the betrothal contract is nonsense."

She summoned her tattered defenses. "Is it, Michel? Is keeping me here against my will also nonsense?"

He trailed a finger along her jawline and a shudder took her. "I'd hardly call it against your will. You want this marriage as much as I do, but you won't admit that what we share is many times more powerful and lasting than your so-called love."

"This is getting us nowhere."

"On the contrary, it's getting us exactly where we need to be. A moment ago you wanted what I could give you so much you could taste it. Even now, you wonder what it will be like. Every sense you possess craves the answer." As he spoke he trailed his hand along the sensitive nape of her neck, lifting her hair slightly until tremors of desire raced down her spine. It was all she could do not to turn her face and press her lips greedily against his palm. "Admit it."

There was only one possible answer. "Yes."

"Then why do you fight it so, *ma amouvere?*"

Heart of my heart. Something turned over inside her as he used the most intimate of the many Carramer terms of endearment. He was seducing her with words as well as kisses and, pity help her, she was a willing accomplice. She did want what he was offering, more than even he knew. She also wanted the place by his side, ruling as his princess and his consort because it meant she would never have to leave.

Was she falling in love with Michel de Marigny?

Bleakness invaded her as she resisted the possibility. None of this was hers by right, and even if it was, she couldn't accept. She meant it when she said she wanted to be loved, above all. However sublime his seduction—and heaven would have little to compare with it, based on what she had already experienced—it was no substitute for love.

"I fight it because I must," she said simply. "Loving involves a lot more than making love."

"Then you will be responsible for my education," he said, a smile to melt stone blossoming on his even features.

It would be an education for two, she felt sure. Temptation beckoned, as strong as anything she'd ever known, but she hardened her heart. "You may have twisted me around your royal finger when we were children, Michel, but it won't work now."

"Are you sure?"

He turned to her with the baby in his arms, and her certainty eroded like a sandbank before a rising tide. She saw him perceive the fact. Luc's expression was alight with pleasure at finding himself beside the sea. The baby leaned toward her eagerly and chuckled as she took him from Michel.

When his baby arms curled around her neck, she melted inside as she was sure the prince meant her to do. She almost said that two against one wasn't fair, but kept her mouth shut. It was bad enough that Michel knew exactly the effect he had on her without his son getting into the act as well. The sooner she got away from them both, the better, she told herself, wondering why she felt less than convinced.

Chapter Eight

The private beach boasted a small cabana and Michel led them to it. Inside it was blissfully cool, the traditional palm-frond roof and wide eaves providing welcome shade.

The cabana consisted of one large room with a food preparation area and a bathroom separated from the lounging area by a low room divider. The main room was furnished with comfortable cane armchairs and low tables, with a cane daybed against one wall. Another wall of glass doors could be slid aside, opening the cabana to a spectacular view of the ocean.

A beautifully carved cradle and high chair suggested that Michel often brought the baby here. She secured the baby into the high chair and gave him a cup of juice from the picnic basket. He gnawed happily on the cup handle.

The prince watched her, his expression unreadable. "Would you also like a cool drink before we swim?" he asked.

The nape of her neck felt damp and she lifted her hair with both hands. "That would be lovely, thank you."

Strange that she could sound so composed, given the turmoil inside her, she thought. It hardly seemed fair that she should feel so shaken by his kisses when Michel himself looked undisturbed. He would have had much more practice at hiding his feelings from public view, she knew, but she hated the thought that she was the only one affected.

"Luc seems to like it here," she commented.

"It is our refuge from palace life."

"Do you need one?"

He cocked a dark eyebrow. "Sometimes the pressure of being royal grows onerous. Not the duties themselves but the need to live up to the expectations of so many people."

Like her? she couldn't help thinking. "You mean here you can let your hair down."

"The Carramer expression is 'kick your toes in the sand,'" he explained with a wry smile.

His mood was infectious and she found herself smiling back. "For that, you would first have to remove your shoes."

Without another word he kicked off his sandals and picked up the drink he had poured for her, padding barefoot across the tiled floor to bring it to her. For a second her heart almost stopped. It was as if he had shed his royal persona with the sandals, and now came to her as an ordinary man.

She accepted the drink, careful not to let her fingers brush his. Sensitized as she was to him, it wouldn't take much more for her to fall into his arms again. The cabana was far too secluded to take the risk.

Then he startled her by dropping to one knee beside her chair. Before she could ask what he was doing, he had slid her shoes off so she was also barefoot. He kept one foot cupped in his hand, massaging it with slow, seductive movements.

Unwilling pleasure spiraled through her and she hastily put the drink down. She could hardly breathe. When he released one foot and began on the other, something melted inside her. She made herself draw away from his grasp. "Don't, please."

"It can't be because you don't like it. A moment ago you were practically purring."

"Well, I don't like it," she snapped, annoyed with herself for being so transparent. Staying in character as Eleanor was becoming harder and harder. She tried to sound petulant and suspected she failed. "I don't like any of this. I want to go home to America."

A dark, shuttered look came over him and he stood up abruptly. "I see. You still have not accepted that America is no longer your home."

"How can I accept it when it's obvious that you only want to marry for convenience's sake?"

He prowled across the room, stooping to retrieve Luc's dropped rattle, clean it and return it to its owner. Then he swung around. "You seem very sure it's my reason."

"Isn't it? Or is it that you're still so in love with Luc's mother that you have no room for anyone else in your life?"

Horror shook her. She hadn't meant to say any such thing, but it was too late to retract her thoughtless words. She didn't even know whether or not they were true.

"You find palace gossip more reliable than my word?"

"No, I...oh, Michel, I'm sorry. I didn't mean to say that."

"But it was in your thoughts. Perhaps it is as well that we—what do you Americans say?—clear the air before we are married."

"There's no need, really." It was one thing to assume that he was still carrying a torch for Luc's mother and quite another to hear it from Michel himself. She wasn't sure she was ready for this.

His expression was carved from stone. "Evidently there is a need. You have made up your mind that I am bringing Luc up alone because I am still mourning his mother. Nothing could be further from the truth."

This was costing him a great deal, she saw with a rush of anguish. Was it the first time he had spoken to anyone about his relationship with the baby's mother? Caroline hadn't meant to force him into any sort of confession and she regretted bitterly that she had spoken so rashly, but she couldn't think of a way to undo the damage. "You don't have to tell me anything if you'd rather not," she assured him. "It's none of my business."

"As my wife, everything that concerns me also concerns you," he stated in such a bleak voice that she felt chilled at the sound of it. Whatever she was about to learn, it was at the cost of his goodwill toward her, she accepted as her spirits plunged. She had asked for this, but she would give almost anything not to have to hear it if it meant that Michel would speak to her so coldly from now on.

The prince began to pace, the cabana barely accommodating his long-legged strides. "The truth is, Luc's mother was a distant member of the royal family, serving as a member of my staff. After becoming pregnant to a tourist who had left the kingdom, she discovered that she was dying of a rare brain disorder and would not live long past her baby's birth. She begged me to find a loving family to adopt the baby and it was then I decided to become his father myself. I allowed the rumor to spread that I was his natural father, to protect her and Luc."

"Not many men would take in an orphaned child and bring him up as their own," she said, her voice catching. It wasn't the explanation she had expected and she had trouble absorbing the discovery that Luc wasn't Michel's love child after all.

His harsh glance raked her. "It wasn't noble, it was selfish," he countered. "I wanted very much to be a father. Lorne had already taken care of the succession, so for once, I was able to please myself."

"So you let everyone think Luc is yours." It was a high price to pay for the baby's sake, and she couldn't help but admire Michel for his willingness to pay it.

"Not everyone. My family knows the truth and have agreed to support me for Luc's sake," he pointed out. "This way he has the protection of my name and property if anything should happen to me, and he will be accepted in society without having fingers pointed at him."

"You've ensured that the fingers point at you instead?"

His broad shoulders lifted. "It's of no consequence. The tabloid press portray me as a playboy now, on very little evidence. Having a love child only serves to confirm what they believe already, although they don't know the whole story and I don't plan on enlightening them. The image has its uses as a smoke screen against predatory women, and I'm far less vulnerable than Luc."

But he was still vulnerable, she sensed. How lucky Luc was to have such a father. And his people to have such a prince. "Will you tell Luc the truth?"

"As he grows I will tell him whatever he is able to understand, but in the meantime he will have the protection of my name while he is least able to protect himself."

It was such an incredibly generous act that she began to wonder if she knew Michel as well as she had thought. When they were children, he had always been willing to share whatever he had and to be available when she needed his help, however busy he was. Now she saw that the tendency had only deepened in the man he had become.

"Are you satisfied now?" he demanded, breaking into her thoughts.

In the face of his disdain, she quailed inwardly. It was as if by driving him to explain Luc's parentage, she had destroyed some bridge they had barely begun to build between them. She felt heartbroken. She had known she would lose Michel's goodwill once he learned about her deception, but she hadn't expected it to happen so soon and over something so unexpected.

"I'm sorry I forced you into discussing such a painful subject," she said quietly. "But I admire your decision more than I can say."

"We don't need your admiration or your understanding," he denied fiercely. He strode to the high chair and gently lifted the baby out of it, cradling Luc against the hard wall of his chest. The sight of the big man holding the adorable baby boy threatened to trigger almost overwhelming feelings of longing inside her, until she fought them down.

The prince seemed unaware of her internal battle. "Luc is now my son in every way that matters. If you mention this conversation to anyone other than my immediate family, I shall deny that it ever took place."

Hurt beyond words, she blinked furiously to dispel the mist clouding her vision. "You must have a low opinion of me if you think such a caution is necessary."

"With the exception of my duty to my people, Luc's welfare comes before everything—including your feelings," he said tautly.

She had hurt him by forcing the admission from him, she saw from Michel's bleak, dark gaze. What it meant about their relationship, if she could hurt him on such a level, she didn't want to consider so she took refuge in anger of her own. "Surely this shows more than ever how incompatible we are?"

At her sharp tone, the baby whimpered in protest and Michel lifted him against his shoulder, rubbing Luc's small back reassuringly. He spoke in Carramer, but Caroline's heart ached as she recognized his words of comfort. She didn't begrudge the baby Michel's attention, but it served to illustrate the emptiness of her own life. She had her work and a circle of friends, but where was the love? Where was her prince? The baby of her own? "Why don't you let me go?" she asked on a note of appeal.

For a long moment, his gaze transfixed her over the baby's downy head. "Because I don't think you really want me to," he said at last.

Could it possibly be true? She refused to acknowledge that the ache inside her had anything to do with wanting Michel to regard her with the same gentleness and love as he did his son. The thought was almost more than she could deal with. She spun away before he could see the tears clouding her eyes that pride refused to let her shed.

"Where are you going?" he demanded.

"To change."

"Don't go into the sea without me or one of the guards. These waters can be dangerous."

Not as dangerous as remaining in the same room with Michel, she thought, and closed the bathroom door between them. If Michel wasn't mourning Luc's mother, except as an employee and the mother of his son, why was he so determined to hold her to a marriage of convenience? There had to be more to this than Michel was prepared to tell her.

Telling herself she needed to know the rest for Eleanor's sake, Caroline wasn't sure she believed it. Her twin had no intention of coming to Carramer and marrying Michel, so there was no reason for Caroline to concern herself with the prince's affairs. She would be far better off using her energy to figure a way out of here.

Since she wasn't going to manage it now, with Michel's bodyguards watching the cabana from a discreet distance, she might as well swim after all. Moments later, surveying herself in Eleanor's borrowed gold bikini in the full-length bathroom mirror, Caroline was shocked at how revealing it was. There had been no opportunity to shop for something more modest, and Eleanor had refused to allow her to pack her white maillot. Luckily the bathroom was well supplied with fluffy white towels so Caroline wound one around herself sarong-style before stepping back into the main room.

She needn't have worried. In the interval while she changed, Michel had stretched out on the daybed and, with the baby safely nestled between the wall and his body, both were fast asleep.

She stopped short, feeling her breath becoming fast and shallow as she watched them. A prince he might be, but asleep with the baby curled into the crook of his arm, Michel looked like every father since time immemorial.

He must have had a difficult morning, she thought, her conscience troubled. She knew how much of himself he gave to his people. Why had she chosen one of his few times for relaxation to push him on the question of Luc's mother? She regretted it bitterly but knew there was no going back.

Already she missed the warmth that had begun to flare between them. She missed the stirring passion of his kisses, she admitted to herself. What other bridges had she burned by speaking out of turn? Seeing Michel and the baby asleep together reminded her powerfully of all she yearned for in her own life.

Blinking hard, she pushed her feet back into her sandals and tiptoed out of the cabana.

Mindful of Michel's warning that the sea could be treacherous, she headed for a lagoon at one end of the beach. It was partially shaded and the water felt like silk as she waded in up to her thighs. With a sigh, she slid in all the way and floated onto her back, letting the water buoy her.

She floated for what seemed like hours, until the sound of babyish giggles caught her attention. She rolled over and trod water, looking for the source of the sounds. Michel had changed into black swimming trunks and was swishing the baby through the shallow water at the edge of the lagoon. Luc gurgled with delight.

Watching them, she felt a resurgence of the fierce need that had gripped her in the cabana. For the first time since arriving in Carramer, she felt like an outsider. Would she ever feel like she truly belonged here?

She decided she owed it to herself to try to repair the damage. Swimming sidestroke, she caught up with Michel and the baby in the shallows. "Michel, I want to apologize," she began awkwardly.

"There's no need," he assured her, his cool tone suggesting otherwise.

"Yes, there is. I shouldn't have asked you to explain your relationship with Luc's mother."

"Granted," the prince agreed. "I should have offered the explanation myself before you were forced to ask."

Frustration gnawed at her. "That isn't what I meant. Oh, for goodness' sake, can't we pretend the conversation never happened?"

He seemed genuinely puzzled. "Why would you do that?"

"Because…" About to say that she wanted them to go back to the way they were before, she stopped herself. Did she really want to admit how much she wanted his warmth, his passion—his love? "I don't want to quarrel with you," she finished lamely.

Sitting in the shallows, he jiggled the baby up and down

on his bent knees. "Believe me, I would rather not quarrel with you," he said over Luc's happy cries.

"Then you forgive me?"

His gaze met hers over the baby's head. "Forgiveness implies a fault on your part. I have already said that the fault was mine."

He was so determined to be civilized that she felt her anger building. If he hadn't been holding the baby, she would have pushed him backward into the water. Never mind if it was a capital crime in Carramer. She was past caring. "Are you always this hard to get along with?" she asked furiously.

Answering sparks flew from the look he directed her way. "If it wasn't for Luc, I would gladly show you how hard I can be," he said, his meaning unmistakable.

Despite the coolness of the water she felt herself growing hot. His gaze dropped to the swelling of her breasts emphasized by the brevity of the bikini top. She resisted the temptation to cover herself with her hands or sink lower in the water. "Then I should be thankful for small mercies," she said with a meaningful look at Luc.

The prince redirected his glance to the baby. "What do you think, Luc? Would you like to get to know your new mother better?"

As if he understood the question, Luc squirmed toward Caroline, holding out two chubby arms to her. She took him from the prince without a second thought. "You like this, don't you?" she said to the baby as she trickled water over his exposed tummy.

He gurgled approvingly and when she did it again, he clapped his hands. Her heart melted. She was so engrossed in amusing the baby that she almost forgot Michel watching them until he murmured approvingly, "You're good at this."

"El...Caroline and I got a lot of practice handling babies when we lived in various villages around the South Pacific," she confessed, unnerved at how she had almost blurted out the wrong name.

Thankfully the prince didn't seem to notice. "You're a natural mother. It bodes well for when we have children of our own."

She was so shocked that she almost allowed Luc to slip off her knee into the water, until she made an effort to regain her composure. The baby thought it was part of the game and chuckled happily. "What makes you so sure we will have children?"

"It's the natural consequence when two people make love," he pointed out.

"I know that. I just didn't think—"

"You didn't think I would expect children from a marriage such as ours?" he cut across her. "I never intended that Luc should be an only child."

"But children should be born into an atmosphere of love, not the kind of loveless arrangement you propose," she said, feeling her pulse pick up speed at the very idea of bearing his children. He would have discovered her identity long before such a thing could happen, but she couldn't help the instinctive cramping of her womb that accompanied the thought.

He looped his arms around his bent knees. "In Carramer, royal children have been born into arranged marriages for centuries and have been loved and cherished for their own sakes. Are you saying you don't want to have my children?"

She couldn't make herself say it when the very opposite was true. Alone with him in the idyllic lagoon setting, with his adopted son in her arms, she knew she wanted to have his children more than anything in the world. But she couldn't admit that she didn't have the right, without betraying Eleanor. So she kept silent.

He put his own interpretation on her silence. "I see I have more work to do to change your mind on the matter of children, as well as toward our marriage itself. It seems the sooner I set the official date, the better."

"It won't change anything," she said stubbornly.

"Are you sure?" He leaned over the baby and kissed her full on her parted lips. Coming on top of his vow to give her children, it jump-started her desire in a way she hadn't anticipated and didn't want to experience.

Her body took little notice. A riot of sensations tore through her, overwhelming in their intensity. If not for the baby in her arms, she would have jumped out of the water and run as far and as fast as she could from Michel.

Away from him or away from herself, her customary honesty forced her to ask. She was afraid she knew the answer and if it was true, it was vital that she contact the Sloanes as soon as she could and ask them to help her escape from Carramer. Too bad they couldn't help her to escape from her own feelings.

Chapter Nine

She had almost given up hope of contacting the Sloanes before Michel publicly announced their wedding, when he came to her suite to deliver the news.

"We are dining aboard *Sargasso* this evening. Walter and Mildred asked me to tell you how much they look forward to seeing you again. They only regret that it is the night before they are due to sail."

"I regret that, too," she said and meant it, because it would also be the last time she would see Michel. If all went well, she would be with the Sloanes when they left in the morning. By the time the prince realized what she had done, they would be outside Carramer territorial waters and he would be powerless to bring her back.

She should feel cheered by the prospect, she told herself. Instead she felt weighed down by something she refused to own as regret. And a deeper feeling that she didn't want to examine at all. It felt too new and tender. Instinctively she knew if she touched it, she was lost.

"What are you doing?" he asked.

She started. She had been sorting Eleanor's possessions, trying to decide what she could safely take with her aboard *Sargasso*. Very little, if she wasn't to arouse Michel's suspicion, she had decided. "Tidying," she lied.

He took an almost transparent nightgown from her hands and looked at it for a moment, as if picturing her wearing it. With what she could swear was regret, he let it float on to the bed. "You have a maid to do that."

The instant his fingers brushed hers, a jolt like summer lighting arced through her, forcing her breathing to quicken. "I like to be useful," she insisted, the hoarseness in her voice a betrayal in itself.

He heard it. "There are many ways you can be useful."

His head was close to hers, his mouth a tantalizing few inches away. She held her breath, wanting him to kiss her and fearing it would only drag her into deeper emotional water. Instead, he drew back with every sign of reluctance. "The cabinet is waiting for me." He straightened as if it cost him. "I want them to know about our forthcoming marriage before I announce it publicly."

She swallowed hard. "Do they know about the betrothal contract?"

"A few of the older statesmen do, those who served under my father. They are traditionalists and would prefer me to marry a woman of Carramer."

"Then perhaps you should."

His wonderful, sensuous mouth hardened. "They also honor the tradition of the betrothal. For some of them it creates something of a dilemma."

"Not only for them," she murmured.

He brushed a few strands of hair off her forehead. "Still, you fight it. But not for much longer. Tomorrow I will make the official announcement."

Shock coiled through her. "So soon?"

His lips followed the path of his hand, burning a trail across her forehead, and she felt a shock of a different kind. "Not nearly soon enough, *ma amouvere*." He drew away with an obvious effort. "I will meet you tonight aboard *Sargasso*."

"We won't go together?"

"My work may delay me. If you go on ahead, I won't be responsible for keeping you apart from your friends."

His thoughtfulness touched her even as guilt welled up. "Thank you, Michel." On impulse she lifted herself onto tiptoes and brushed a kiss across his cheek. "You've been good to me."

His eyes darkened and a frown hovered, then was banished. "You make it sound as if it's over when it has barely begun."

If only it were true, she thought as the door closed behind him. But it was over, it had to be. Michel's contract was with Eleanor. There was no place for Caroline in his life. She should be grateful that he had simplified things by letting her go on ahead to meet the Sloanes. So why did she feel as if she was betraying the prince?

The *Sargasso* looked little changed since Caroline had lived aboard it in her teens. The 66-foot ketch was built from New Zealand kauri, teak, silver ash, rosewood and mahogany with brass fittings, and had seen service as an air-rescue vessel during the Second World War, then as a radio relay ship for oceangoing yacht races before the Sloanes converted her to a research vessel. Like their boat, Walter and Mildred looked amazingly well, and Caroline assumed it was the joy they took in their work.

After they exchanged hugs, Walter led the way down to a cluttered saloon out of sight of Michel's security people who had been detailed to accompany Caroline.

Walter held Caroline at arm's length. "No doubt about it, you've blossomed into a beautiful woman, Eleanor."

She frowned. "I have something to tell you before Michel arrives." She dragged in a deep breath. "In the first place, I'm not Eleanor, I'm Caroline."

Walter looked startled. "I would never have guessed. Does Prince Michel know?"

She shook her head. "It's the reason I need your help." Haltingly she told them everything, ending with Eleanor's engagement to Darmy. "So you see why I had to take her place?"

Mildred nodded. "I see it's a terrible mix-up. That father of yours ought to be shot for getting you girls into this."

Caroline smiled wanly. "He meant well, but it doesn't change the outcome. Will you help get me away from Michel?"

"I don't know," Walter began, massaging his short gray beard.

Mildred silenced him with a look. "Of course we will, honey. The only thing is, how will you get him to let you stay on board after dinner?"

The question had troubled Caroline, too. "I could pretend to be ill."

Walter shook his head. "He'd whisk you to the palace doctor so fast your head would spin."

"We could just invite her to stay the night," Mildred suggested to her husband. "The prince knows we're old friends. He wouldn't find it suspicious."

"Except for the fact that we're casting off at dawn."

Caroline felt her shoulders slump and lifted them resolutely. "There is one possibility. If I was drunk, he'd have to leave me here to sleep it off."

"But you drink very little, honey. Won't he think it's odd if you suddenly start?"

Caroline shook her head. "He thinks I'm Eleanor, remember?"

Walter made a face. "Now why am I not surprised that she turned into a party animal? I recall when she insisted on sampling my whisky although she was underage. I said no but she kept at me until I told her to go ahead, take a good swallow. Her face was a study. You'd think I'd tried to poison her."

Mildred frowned. "Evidently it wasn't as much of a deterrent as it should have been."

Caroline shifted uncomfortably. "It's not as bad as it sounds. Eleanor and I have different life-styles, that's all. She plays hard, but she works hard as well and she's there for me when I need her."

Mildred's hand sought hers. "Then why is she off pleasing herself while you deal with her problem?"

"If our roles were reversed, she would do the same for me," Caroline insisted loyally. She shot a nervous glance at the ship's chronometer. "Michel should be here soon."

"Then we'd better get organized," Walter interpreted, standing up. "I'll open a couple of bottles of wine and pour one of them down the sink so it'll look like the party's already started. Don't worry," he said, catching her anxious look. "I won't waste any good stuff."

"The prince will take it hard when he finds out you're gone," Mildred said gently, as her husband bustled about the galley.

Caroline lifted her chin. "Only because he's used to women falling at his feet."

Mildred looked startled. "Where did you get that notion?"

"He is known as the playboy prince."

The older woman fiddled with her wire-rimmed glasses.

"Some men play the field to avoid getting hurt by any one woman."

Caroline remembered what Michel had told her about allowing the tabloid press to portray him as a playboy for his own purpose, although there was little substance to it. She began to wonder if Mildred was right.

When she suggested this, Mildred shook her head. "I don't know about that, but I do know the prince had a bad experience with his sister-in-law, Chandra."

Caroline's head came up. "Lorne's late wife?"

"That's her, and a fine piece of goods she was, by all accounts. Michel told me about it over drinks late one night. We'd been up for hours correlating data on the frequency of pattern recognition in the dolphin pod and I guess we were all exhausted. I asked why a fine man like him was still single. Maybe it was the wine or the tiredness but he finally opened up about how Chandra had come on to him pretty strongly one night at his brother's palace. Told him Prince Lorne had forced her into becoming pregnant again. This time she was expecting twins."

"It doesn't sound like the Prince Lorne I used to know."

"Michel thought so, too. When he refused to help her get away, she threatened to tell Lorne that Michel had forced her into his bed."

"Surely Lorne wouldn't believe it?"

"Michel didn't want it to come to that, and risk Lorne wondering for the rest of his life whether Chandra's babies were his or his brother's. Michel decided to try and talk sense into Chandra in a less explosive setting. She crashed her car and was killed on the way to meet him."

Caroline's eyes widened. "Does Lorne know that Chandra was going to meet Michel?"

"No good would come of telling him now. If Michel hadn't agreed, she would have plotted with someone else and the scandal might have damaged the royal house, but it doesn't stop Michel from blaming himself.''

''And making sure he doesn't leave himself as vulnerable as Lorne did,'' Caroline said. ''But for the accident, Lorne would still be in that disastrous marriage.'' She dragged in a breath. ''No wonder he thinks of love as a trap.''

''Do you still want to go off into the night?''

What else could she do? Whether she stayed or left, Michel would be hurt because of her. Now she couldn't even claim ignorance. ''I have no choice. It would be worse for him to announce our marriage publicly, then find out the truth.''

''Chandra all over again,'' Mildred agreed.

Walter handed her a glass of wine. ''You'd better drink some of this before the prince arrives.'' He set a half-empty bottle on the stand beside her. ''Are you any good at acting drunk?''

''I've never tried.''

''Then best you pretend to be sleepy, as if you can barely keep your eyes open. Act as if everything's funny, even when it's not.''

She nodded, wondering how anyone could let themselves get into such a state. ''I know you disapprove, Walter, but I appreciate your help. I'm only sorry to have to put you in this position.''

He nodded. ''I've never turned away a friend in need yet, and you were always willing to help us with our work. You've earned my support.''

She sighed with relief. ''I loved helping you. Your work fascinated me and still does. Are you any closer to communicating with the dolphins?''

Mildred's eyes sparkled. ''We know they can recognize and remember shapes so we've evolved a system of symbols and an underwater touch screen to help us interact with them.''

''Can they see a video screen?''

Walter nodded. ''When we show them a video of some-one feeding dolphins, they try to catch the fish, proving they see the screen the same way we do. Between our system of infra-ray transmitters, sensors and the touch screen, we'll soon be able to exchange information with them, such as the call signs they use to identify themselves.''

''They have names for each other?''

''Just like we do.''

''How can you leave it if you're close to a break-through?'' Caroline asked.

''We'll continue our work in Florida, but we also need to communicate with each other, something that we've ne-glected in favor of the dolphins,'' Mildred said with a rueful glance at her husband.

''Forty-three years we've been married,'' he volunteered. ''Forty of 'em spent at sea or under it. I want my wife to myself on dry land for a while.''

An ache started inside Caroline. The strength of the bond between Walter and Mildred emphasized her own solitary state. They had each other. Eleanor had Danny. Who was for her? Not Michel came the swift conviction and with it a sense of emptiness. She hated to fuel his mistrust of women, but by forcing her to stay, he had left her no option.

Desperation gave her the strength to pretend she'd been drinking when Michel finally arrived. When Walter and Mil-dred rose in deference to the prince, she remained stub-bornly seated. She even managed to giggle as the prince apologized to Walter and Mildred for being delayed by af-fairs of state. He shot her a regal glare. ''What is so amus-ing?''

''You, my prince,'' she said, remembering to slur her

words slightly. She waved a half-empty wineglass in the air. "Princes shouldn't have affairs, even affairs of state."

She saw that his expression barely altered. Royal training, she assumed and tried not to flinch from the look in his eyes. He looked stunned, as if this was the last thing he had expected from her.

She blundered on. "We did as you asked and started without you."

A muscle worked along his jaw. "So I see. It might help if you eat something."

Mildred got up. "If you're ready, I'll serve dinner now, Your Highness."

He inclined his head slightly. "It's still Michel, and thank you, Mildred."

If Caroline had endured a worse dining experience, she couldn't recall. Michel was clearly troubled as she pretended to down several more glasses of wine in quick succession while eating almost nothing of the excellent crab Mornay Mildred had prepared. Unbeknownst to Michel, the potted plant at Caroline's side was the beneficiary of most of the wine. It would probably survive the experience better than she would, she thought miserably.

Several times Michel tried to dissuade her from refilling her glass, offering her chilled springwater instead. She would have loved some to rid her mouth of its cotton-wool feeling, but she made herself refuse airily. "I like Carramer wine. It's strong and full-bodied, like Carramer men," she burbled.

Walter and Mildred tried valiantly to keep up a normal conversation and Michel contributed through clenched teeth. By the time coffee was served, Caroline was so nervous that spilling wine onto the tablecloth wasn't an act. She fumbled the glass as she tried to set it on the table.

Michel caught the empty glass before it crashed to the

deck. "It's time for us to return to the palace," he said, getting to his feet.

She made a show of rising, only to collapse in her seat again.

Mildred looked genuinely concerned. "Why don't I put her to bed here? You can have your driver collect her before we leave tomorrow."

The prince smiled but no humor reached his eyes. "It might be better than the scene we are likely to create if I try to get her to the car. Are you sure it's no trouble?"

"Of course not. I'm only sorry our stay has to end like this."

His hard look softened slightly. "It isn't your fault. Working with you and Walter has enriched my understanding of marine biology immeasurably. I wish you both a safe journey home to America and a pleasant retirement."

"Safe journey," Caroline echoed thickly. If he only knew.

She wanted to weep but forced herself to smile stupidly as Michel bid them goodnight. She waited until she heard his car pull away before she straightened and pushed the wineglass away with a grimace.

"Looks like your plan worked," Walter commented.

Thinking of Michel's set face, she would almost have preferred that it failed. "Apparently."

Mildred put an arm around her shoulder. "You don't look too happy about it, honey. You know we care about you and you're most welcome to sail with us, as long as you're sure it's what you want to do."

What she wanted and what she had to do were two different things. She nodded wordlessly. By this time tomorrow she would be on her way back to America and this would be over.

Over.

If she had felt empty before, it was nothing compared to the abyss yawning inside her now. Thinking of Michel's reaction as he watched her apparently drink herself insensible, she felt drained of any sense of victory. It hurt that he would always remember her like this, while she had to live with the bittersweet memory of his arms around her and his kisses driving her to the brink of reason.

She stood up, adjusting her stance to the boat's gentle rocking. "I'll help you clean up before I turn in."

Mildred stayed her with a hand on her arm. "I'll do it, honey. You look all in. Tonight was hard for you, wasn't it?"

"Harder for Michel."

"But you're the one who loves him," Mildred said.

The older woman did not say that Michel loved *her*, Caroline noted. In an instant she knew it was true. Michel might not love her, but she loved him with all her heart. "Yes," she admitted softly, knowing it was true and had been for some time.

When had she fallen in love with the prince? When he first took her in his arms? When he kissed her to prove his mastery over her on the beach? Or so long ago that she couldn't recall a time when she *hadn't* loved Michel de Marigny?

Mildred's look was filled with compassion as she read the truth in Caroline's expression. "I thought as much. He's betrothed to your sister, yet you're the one who's in love with him. No wonder you feel you need to get away."

Wordlessly Walter set a steaming mug of coffee in front of her and she cupped her hands around it, letting her shoulders sag. "Thanks—for everything."

He squeezed her shoulder. "I don't approve of any of this, but neither can I stand by and see you suffer. Mildred would have my head."

His wife regarded him with fierce affection. "You got that right. Now go make up a cabin for our guest."

Walter disappeared below and Caroline nursed the coffee while the older woman bustled around, setting the galley to rights. She refused Caroline's repeated offer to help, insisting it was enough to have the company. "Your cabin will be ready soon, dear, then you can get a good night's rest. Everything will look better in the morning."

Caroline doubted it but nodded. She jumped when the cruiser's radio telephone squawked for attention, watching listlessly as Mildred answered it. "She's asleep," she said with a quick glance at Caroline, and a finger pressed to her lips. "I'll be sure and tell her. Is there anything I can do?"

A worried note in Mildred's voice alerted Caroline and she sat up straighter, waiting tensely until Mildred replaced the receiver. "There's something wrong with Michel, isn't there?"

Mildred laced her fingers together. "Not with the prince, with his little boy. Soon after Prince Michel returned to the palace, the baby was taken ill and rushed to the hospital. The prince thought you should be told where he is in case you needed to reach him."

Coldness invaded Caroline as she pictured the adorable infant lying helpless in a hospital bed. "What's wrong with Luc?"

"Evidently he was feverish and convulsing and lost consciousness for a minute, so the hospital admitted him for observation."

Caroline levered herself away from the table. "I have to go to them."

Mildred chewed her lip. "Are you sure? Walter and I have to sail tomorrow. We have commitments back in the States, or we'd wait for you."

"I understand but I can't leave him at a time like this."

Mildred seemed to understand that Caroline meant the prince as much as the baby. Both needed her now. She could no more sail away from them than she could fly under her own power. Woodenly, she gathered the few things she'd brought with her.

The older woman picked up the radio telephone and spoke into it. "The palace is sending a car to take you to the hospital." She hung up and enveloped Caroline in a motherly embrace. "If it helps, I think you're doing the right thing."

Caroline's throat felt arid. "I'm doing the only thing. Michel needs me. Nothing else matters."

Mildred gave a wan smile. "That's love for you. Is there anything Walter and I can do?"

"You've done more than enough. Have a safe journey home."

A polite rap on the cabin door told them the palace driver had arrived. Caroline hugged her friend quickly then turned away, her vision misty. She barely heard Mildred's injunction to call and let her know how things worked out, but she managed to nod.

The drive to the hospital passed in a blur. Never had Caroline been so thankful for royal privilege as a path was cleared for the car all the way to the hospital where she was taken directly to the emergency entrance, and a hospital official delegated to steer her to the private wing where Luc had been admitted.

"How is the baby?" she asked as she strove to keep up with the official's brisk pace.

"As well as can be expected," came the unhelpful reply. "The royal pediatrician is attending him and will be able to tell you more."

She was left at the door of a private waiting room that bore little resemblance to the hospital rooms of her experience. It looked more like a luxury hotel suite, with every comfort anticipated. She barely absorbed the details as her attention was riveted by the sight of the tall man pacing the plush carpeting in front of her. "Michel."

Her voice startled him out of some reverie, but his reaction wasn't what she had expected. "What are you doing here?"

"Mildred told me about Luc. I had to come."

The prince's hard gaze bored into her. "Why?"

"I care about you, both of you," she added hastily. "How could I l-lie there and let you deal with this alone?" She had been about to say "leave," stopping herself barely in time.

He faced her flatly. "Interesting that you should use the word 'lie.' Does your caring come into that category?"

Her heart felt as if it was being squeezed in a vise. "You think I'm lying about this?"

"Why not? You've had plenty of practice at it lately."

The floor felt as if it had dropped away from under her feet. She groped for the wall and rested against it. "What do you mean?"

"Must I spell it out for you...Caroline?"

Her voice came out low and strained. "How long have you known?"

He gave a humorless smile. "No denials? No protestations?"

"No point, obviously," she countered, her thoughts spinning. Had he known when he kissed her that she wasn't Eleanor?

He read her thoughts as if they were written out for him. "Now you wonder who I kissed—you or your twin? And was it passion or punishment? You may never know for sure."

"Hurt me as I've hurt you?" she queried. "Is that the

plan, Michel? Because if it is, I never meant to hurt you. You must believe me.''

His expression contorted into a sneer. ''Why should I, when you've shown such skill at twisting the truth?''

''Because I'm here.''

The simple statement was unrehearsed, but as soon as she said it, she knew it was true. In giving up her chance to escape, she had known she would have to tell Michel the truth, or at least the part of it that concerned him. Her feelings were her own affair. There was no need to burden him with her love. Keeping silent would be her penance for deceiving him.

''I see you have recovered from your…indisposition.''

She sighed, guessing from his tone that he knew this was an act, too. She studied him curiously. ''If you knew I wasn't really drunk, why did you let me remain aboard the boat?''

''To see what you would do.''

''And if I had left with Walter and Mildred?''

''Then you would be gone.''

She couldn't tell from his tone whether this would have pleased him or not and she assumed it was no accident. Plainly Michel intended to tell her only what he wished her to know. He had managed to keep from her his knowledge of her deception. What else might he be concealing from her? Better not to raise any foolish hopes, she warned herself. ''What gave me away?'' she asked in a low voice.

His long fingers flexed as if he would like to break something, possibly her. ''I was suspicious from the first. Then I found you in my private garden, cradling my son, although you had no idea who he was. I knew Eleanor would never behave so tenderly toward a strange child. You may be your sister's mirror image, but you cannot imitate her nature. Years ago she tried to pose as you so I would take her to see the dolphins. I allowed her to think I was fooled, but I wasn't. Even as a child, she was vain and self-centered, more interested in enjoying herself than in caring for others."

Was he saying she *wasn't* vain or self-centered? Caroline felt foolishly cheered by the compliment, however indirect. She also felt unreasonably pleased that he had never mistaken Eleanor for her. It didn't begin to compensate for the anger she felt emanating from him like a volcano preparing to erupt, but it was something. She released her breath in a rush. "Michel, I'm sorry."

One dark eyebrow lifted. "Because I found you out?"

She spread her hands wide. "Because I've thought of you as my friend since we were children. I hated deceiving you."

"You managed it surprisingly well."

There was no getting away from it. "I know, but I wanted to tell you who I was right from the beginning." You could say her heart was in it, she thought but didn't add. Even if he believed her, he wouldn't want to hear it now, if ever. After what Mildred had told her about the way his sister-in-law had tried to involve him in betraying his brother, Caroline couldn't blame him for rejecting love, but neither could she help her own feelings toward him.

They were interrupted by the arrival of a woman in a white coat, a stethoscope slung around her neck. "I'm Leah Markham, Luc's pediatrician," she told Caroline, offering her hand. To Michel, she said, "Your Highness, we've established that the baby's convulsion is due to a viral respiratory infection."

Michel stepped forward. "The treatment?"

"Already taking effect, sir. While we treat the infection, we have him on extra oxygen and fluids to prevent dehydration." She smiled encouragingly. "Chest infections are common in infants, but Luc is a sturdy little boy and he's getting the best of care."

Michel's expression lightened a little. "I never doubted it."

"The baby is sleeping now and in no danger, so why don't you go home and get some rest, Your Highness?" The doctor's look included Caroline. "Luc will need you more tomorrow. You can look in on him for a few minutes before you go."

With obvious reluctance, Michel nodded. "We'll take your advice. Thank you, Doctor Markham."

As he took Caroline's arm, a pang shot through her. Since hearing of Luc's illness, she hadn't thought past the need to be with Michel and help him through the crisis. Now it was over, what would happen to her? He would probably bundle her aboard the next flight out and good riddance, she thought, her spirits plunging.

Strange how the prospect of being sent away in disgrace should make her feel so wretched, she thought. A few hours ago she had been prepared to sail away under cover of darkness. But that hadn't felt right, either. The simple truth was, everything she cared about was right here. If she left now, a piece of her would always remain behind.

She went with Michel to look in on Luc. The baby looked so tiny and helpless amid the maze of medical equipment, but the nurse watching over him assured them that all would be well. As Michel touched the lightest kiss to the baby's forehead, Caroline's heart tightened with love for them both.

Afterward, they were escorted through the dimly lit corridors to Michel's waiting limousine. The interior was also dark, and as soon as they were inside he depressed a control that partitioned the driver behind soundproof tinted glass. She found she was holding her breath and forced herself to release it. "What happens now?"

"We take the doctor's advice and return to the palace," the prince said evenly.

"I mean afterward, now that you know about me?"

"What do you think should happen?"

He wanted her to name her own punishment? She couldn't see his expression in the darkness, only the devilish gleam lighting his eyes. Didn't he know that a life without him was already the worst punishment she could imagine? She was forced to imagine it now. "I'll leave as soon as we know that Luc is completely out of danger," she said, her voice a croaky parody of herself.

"I'm afraid not."

The single word cut across her like a whip crack. She jerked her head up. "You don't want me to go?"

"That's not the issue," he said as coldly as she had ever heard him speak. He was the prince now, with a thousand years of royal tradition behind him, making his every word law. "There is still the matter of the betrothal contract."

Bitterness welled up inside her. "That stupid contract was the cause of all this."

"That stupid contract, as you call it, will be enforced between us as quickly as I can arrange it."

She was glad he couldn't see her confusion. "How can it be? You are betrothed to Eleanor, not me."

"Irrelevant. You came to me in her place. You will marry me in her place."

Her thoughts whirled. "You mean some kind of proxy wedding?"

"They are not uncommon in Carramer."

The steel in his voice warned her that any argument she offered stood no chance. She had never dreamed that he could elect her as Eleanor's proxy. To have and to hold— but in trust for another? Could she possibly imagine a more dreadful fate? "But Eleanor is in love with another man.

They plan to marry. She will never come to Carramer,"
Caroline whispered.

The prince half turned to her, and she wondered if he
meant to seal his intention with a kiss. Everything in her
rejected the thought, not because she didn't want it—she
did, almost more than life itself—but because it wasn't hers
by right. It never had been. She had been deluding herself.
Michel had made her face the bitter truth.

He didn't kiss her. He didn't even touch her, and she
wondered if he ever would again. "If she never comes, then
you should resign yourself to a long reign at my side, my
proxy princess," he said.

Then she knew there were worse fates than banishment.
He had just pronounced hers.

Chapter Ten

What on earth was he doing, holding Caroline to a proxy wedding? Michel thought of the stunned expressions on the faces of his cabinet ministers when he broke the news. Their respect for his rank and title had kept them from expressing their consternation, but he had seen the question in their eyes—had their prince finally lost his mind?

Only his brother, Lorne, had dared question Michel's judgment aloud during his courtesy visit to the palace at Solano to seek his brother's blessing. "I know I suggested invoking the betrothal contract, but I didn't mean things to go this far. What will you do if Eleanor never agrees to the marriage?" Then the monarch's eyes narrowed in sudden understanding. "You don't want her to agree, do you? Caroline has been the one for you since you were children."

Michel felt a frown etch his brow. "For all the good it has done me."

"She doesn't love you?"

"Her behavior suggests not. In any case, the contract is between Eleanor and me."

"So a proxy marriage lets you legally claim Caroline as your wife," Lorne concluded. "It's a clever strategy."

A hollow one, Michel thought. His suspicion about her real identity had been all but confirmed when he found her working in the conservatory. He had waited for her to confess, but she had not done so, finally choosing to sneak away rather than face him. She was no better than his brother's amoral first wife. Michel had been right to reject what he felt for Caroline. If this was love, he wanted no part of it.

She had changed her mind on hearing that his son was ill, he reminded himself. She could be back in America right now. Instead she was waiting for him on Isle des Anges. She had been genuinely shocked when he told her about the proxy wedding, but she hadn't fought him as he half expected. It made him wonder—no! He slammed a lid on the hope playing havoc with his long-practiced cynicism. How could he trust anything she told him after what she had done?

He could barely trust his own feelings, he acknowledged uncomfortably. He wanted her more than he had ever wanted any woman. In his dreams, she came to him willingly, sharing herself without reservation, trusting him and loving him, until he felt light-headed with love for her.

When he awoke, reality came crashing back. Desire wasn't the same as love. To his eternal regret, he had felt desire for Chandra when she came on to him, although nothing she could have done would have persuaded him to give in to it. But it served as a warning to him not to confuse the two.

So why torture himself by binding Caroline to a union she plainly resented and he feared would undermine his cherished autonomy?

He couldn't let her go. It was as simple as that. No matter how many good reasons he summoned to reject her, part of him refused to consider it. Since the only way he could keep her by his side was through the proxy marriage, that was what he would have.

Lorne clasped his brother's shoulder. "Love is hell, isn't it?"

"I'll let you know when it happens to me."

Lorne gave a sharp laugh. "Resist it all you like, brother, but when it comes to a beautiful face and a gentle nature, a prince is as vulnerable as any man."

From somewhere, Michel found a smile. "The voice of experience?"

"Definitely." Lorne sobered abruptly. "Don't let my experience with Chandra sour you on love, Michel. We've never talked about it before, but I know she did her best to ruin it for you with her scheming."

Michel couldn't hide his shock. "You know about that?"

"I've known all along that she was on her way to meet you when she died. Before she drove away, she taunted me with it, suggesting you had invited the assignation."

Michel felt himself blanch. "Dear heaven, Lorne. I only agreed to meet her to talk sense into her. There was nothing between us, I swear."

"Do you think I don't know you better than that? I can imagine how hard you tried to straighten her out. The point is, she mustn't be allowed to ruin any more lives. Go to Caroline. She deserves another chance. She may have made some mistakes, but she's not Chandra."

The guilt he'd borne over his sister-in-law's death fell away at last. Michel felt a great weight lift from his shoulders. He still wasn't wholly convinced that love was for him, or even that Caroline felt any such thing toward him, but he finally felt as if he could look his brother in the eye again. With his greater experience, if Lorne believed Michel and Caroline had a chance, maybe they had. In spite of everything, he was happily married to Allie. Michel returned Lorne's handclasp firmly. "You're the ruler."

Lorne shook his head. "Not in this. It's strictly between you and Caroline. Do you know what you're going to do?"

Michel's grin felt like his first in a long time. "I intend to follow tradition all the way."

Even Lorne's royal mask slipped a little at this. "Do you mean what I think you mean?"

Michel nodded. "I don't know if what Caroline and I have amounts to love, but there's one way to find out."

"Are you sure it's a good idea?"

"No, but it's the only one I have. Wish me luck."

As he ushered Caroline inside the remote pavilion rising like Brigadoon on an island in the center of the lake, she stared at the prince as if he'd lost his mind. He wasn't sure he hadn't. "You brought me here for *what* reason?"

"According to Carramer tradition, couples spend a night in seclusion together before they marry. Historically, many royal marriages were arranged and the couple had little opportunity to get to know each other before the ceremony, hence the retreat known as a Wedding Eve."

She felt her throat dry but refused to swallow. So this was how he intended to get his revenge. "I suppose you think because I'm Eleanor's proxy, you can do as you like with me," she said coldly. "If you lay a hand on me, I promise you'll live to regret it."

Thinking of the hands he had already laid on her, he couldn't think of a single reason to regret it. But he understood her apprehension. "A Wedding Eve has nothing to do with sex," he said. "Traditionally, the retreat is celibate. It's a chance to get to know each other free of other distractions."

Somehow this prospect was even more alarming. She

tried another tack. "I thought you only meant to show me the pavilion. I didn't bring anything with me."

"Everything you need is here," he assured her.

Truth if ever she heard it. With Michel at her side she needed nothing more. If he were a peasant living in poverty, her feelings wouldn't change. It was why spending a night entirely alone with him was playing with fire. "What about your security people?" she asked, aware of nerves strung as tightly as violin strings.

"They know the tradition and will keep a discreet distance. The causeway we came by is blocked by a high gate linked to the palace security system. The only other access is by water and the island is entirely within the royal estate."

She had seen the details on the way here without absorbing them. She had been too aware of Michel at her side, her husband-to-be, yet as far out of her reach as the moon and the stars. It didn't stop her from wanting him.

Action was called for. "I'd like to look around."

He defied her attempt to get away by coming closer. "We'll do it together. Spending time in each other's company is the whole point of a Wedding Eve."

So much for escape. She tried to focus on her surroundings with little success, far more aware of the man moving sinuously at her side. Distantly she registered that the pavilion was constructed in traditional Carramer style, from hardwoods, bamboos and local fibers in earthen colors. The spacious rooms had contrasting dark timber and white stucco walls, hand-fired tile floors and comfortable rattan furnishings. Beyond a paved terrace, a grove of tiger palms and flowering bushes fringed a swimming pool edged in sandstone and located to take full advantage of the lake view.

"What is the purpose of this place?" she asked. She

dimly recalled asking Shona about the island and being told it was mainly used for charity fund-raising events nowadays.

"Romance," Michel said huskily. "It was built by my great-grandfather for his bride on *their* Wedding Eve."

"Were they happy?"

"Their love was legendary throughout the kingdom. They were married for forty-two years and had seven children."

The contrast with her own situation was almost too much to bear. She blinked to clear her vision. "What are we supposed to do here all night?"

A smile teased his generous mouth. "Get to know each other."

Desolation swept through her. "Why?"

"We are going to be married."

"Not in any real sense."

He touched her chin with one hand, bringing her face up so she was forced to look at him. It was almost her undoing. "We both know Eleanor isn't coming. That leaves you and me."

"It's still a marriage of convenience." She couldn't keep the bitterness out of her voice. "Whatever you call it, it *is* for your convenience, Michel. You get the veneer of respectability your position requires without giving up your playboy ways."

His hands slid to her shoulders, massaging gently. "There has been no one else for a long time."

She tried to ignore the fire spreading from his hands through her body. "Why are you telling me this, Michel?"

"So that you will stop looking at me as the playboy prince, and start thinking of me as a man with a man's normal needs and desires. Unfortunately, being royal means that I cannot always please myself."

She had to know. "Are you pleasing yourself now?"

He dragged in a deep breath and slid his hands away from

her slowly, as if it cost him. "If I was, this wouldn't be a celibate retreat."

The promise in his words fired her with longing. "Look but don't touch?" she tried for a light tone and failed.

He heard it. "It is challenging, but it's the whole point. The physical side is only one aspect of a marriage."

She recalled his reference to Shakespeare's "marriage of true minds," but refused to give in to hope. She was already vulnerable where he was concerned. No point in leaving herself open to more hurt, although she couldn't imagine it getting any worse.

She was wrong.

Being with him every minute, free of the demands of his position, yet being denied more than an occasional touch, was torture of the most exquisite kind. Was this what a proxy marriage would be like? She wondered if he was trying to prepare her.

Well, she was capable of surprising him, too, she thought with sudden resolve. Why not test things to the limit and find out once and for all whether love was as alien to him as he claimed.

The clothes she found in her bedroom made it easier. As evening fell she excused herself long enough to slip into a traditional Carramer *lueur,* so named because it offered a glimpse of tanned flesh beneath flowing silk. The watered fabric was cut in almost Greek lines with a slit to the thigh on each side and a scooped back, the jeweled neckline offering a tantalizing hint of cleavage. A plaited leather belt cinched her waist.

Now she was no longer pretending to be Eleanor, she let her hair flow around her shoulders in her own preferred style, securing it behind one ear with a ginger orchid plucked from a vase in her room.

As she walked into the living room she heard his breath

catch. It was fairly mutual. He had changed into champagne-colored pants and a flowing shirt slashed almost to the waist, making her think of musketeers and pirates. In her absence, a table had been set for two on the open terrace. Delicious aromas emanating from a *bain marie* suggested that the pavilion enjoyed room service from the palace kitchens.

She made her walk as seductive as possible as she went to Michel and accepted the glass of wine he poured for her. With some satisfaction she noted that his hand was less than steady. "Caroline," he said warningly.

Innocence personified, she watched him over the rim of her glass. "What?"

"Whatever it is you're up to, think twice. I believe in tradition but only up to a point."

She allowed her lashes to flutter slightly. "The point being?"

"When I'm provoked beyond endurance."

She widened her eyes. "Don't tell me His Royal Highness, Prince Michel, might actually lose some of his famous control?" Might actually admit that he cared, she thought shakily.

He took the glass from her hand and caught her to him. The touch of skin against skin was incendiary. When his mouth found hers, the room spun. The kiss lasted no more than a few seconds, but it was enough to leave her breathless, with flushed skin and racing heart by the time he moved away. "Are you happy now?"

"No." She came closer, her eyes misting. "I already know you can turn me on, Michel." More than any man on earth, she knew.

"So you decided to return the favor."

"Perhaps I was hoping for something more."

His gaze turned bleak. "There may not be any more. Can't you be content with what I *can* offer?"

"Your name, titles and possessions?" she recited painfully. "If I was Eleanor, it might be enough, but I'm not."

"Then what *do* you want?"

She half turned away so he wouldn't see the hurt she was unable to hide any longer. "More than you are willing to give, apparently."

Anger burned in the fierce gaze he directed at her. "It isn't always a question of willingness."

She swung back. "I know about Chandra, Michel. Mildred Sloane told me what happened between you."

"It was not her place to betray my confidence," he snapped.

"She cares about you," Caroline said, a hairsbreadth from adding, *as I do.*

"Then she must have told you how Chandra proved the futility of this whole love business. My brother loved her, gave her everything, and still it wasn't enough. She betrayed him in the end, hurting him almost beyond recovery."

"Using you as her weapon of choice," Caroline surmised.

He flinched as her shot hit home. "Not an experience easily forgotten."

Or forgiven, she thought, her heart breaking for him. "You can't write off love because of one tragic experience. Lorne didn't, and look how happy he is. I haven't. If I had, I wouldn't be here now."

She hadn't intended to mention Ralph but Michel dismissed her attempt to gloss over the slip. "You were about to say?"

"It doesn't matter."

"When you arrived, you mentioned that 'Caroline' had been betrayed by a lover. What happened?"

She shook her head. "It's over now."

"But not forgotten. I can see the pain in your eyes when you speak of it."

She felt it, too. "His name was Ralph. I...I thought I loved him. One day I came back from a business trip and planned to surprise him by cooking a special meal at his apartment. I was the one surprised because he was already there with another woman."

Michel looked murderous. "They were making love?"

She could hardly speak. "Yes."

He came to her, enveloping her in a hug that held nothing of his earlier passion and everything of comfort and support. She leaned into the embrace with a sense of homecoming. It couldn't last, but Lord knew, she welcomed it now. Ralph's betrayal had hurt but the cure was right here in the arms enfolding her, she sensed. Whatever she had thought she felt before paled into insignificance alongside the feelings that threatened to overwhelm her in Michel's arms.

The prince's voice against her hair sounded husky. "Yet you can still speak of love as one of the seven wonders of the world."

She raised her head. "I suppose you think that makes me an utter fool?"

"I'm probably jealous, that's all."

"Of Ralph?"

Pain shot through Michel. Hell, yes, of course of Ralph for playing the part in Caroline's life that Michel himself coveted. He fought it. "Of your ability to rise above what happened," he ground out.

She moved out of his embrace with an apparent effort that he understood only too well, picked up the wineglass and stared into it for long minutes. "I'm not sure I have risen above it. But if I let him tarnish my belief in love, he wins more than one round. He wins the whole match. I won't let him do that to me."

The fierceness in her tone rocked him. How could he do less than she had set herself to do? "You're a remarkable woman," he said, meaning every word.

Her eyes clouded, making him feel like a brute for forcing her to relive an obviously painful experience. Everything in him longed to make it up to her. In surprise, he realized he wanted to make love to her, not so much to satisfy his own desires as to replace the painful memories with heavenly new ones. Was this what had happened when Lorne met Allie? Startled, Michel wondered when he had started believing in second chances. He suspected the answer was in front of him.

As he escorted her to the table, he noticed how the starlight was reflected in her eyes. Where Caroline was concerned he seemed to notice every little detail. "I hope you don't mind if we serve ourselves. I sent the servants away."

He wanted to be alone with her? She was sure her surprise registered on her face, but when he didn't react, she decided she must be wrong. He probably didn't want the servants reporting on the noticeable lack of romance between the supposedly happy couple. The thought almost tore her apart until she reminded herself that this was the very thing she wanted to test.

As she ladled perfectly chilled lettuce soup from a tureen into Meissen china bowls, he let his eyes wander over the vision she presented. In the traditional Carramer *lueur,* she looked more womanly, more desirable than in anything she had worn before. He felt his body begin to respond and had to strive for the return of control. It was more than her appearance, he knew. Her inner strength inspired and fascinated him. How could anyone so vulnerable be so strong? The same force that enabled women to transcend the agony of childbirth and turn it into a triumphal experience, he thought with another quick flaring of jealousy. He had never wanted her more than he did at that moment.

"You must show me how to maintain my optimism against such odds," he suggested, irony in his tone.

She heard it and flinched. "I would, if I thought you really wanted to know."

"What makes you so sure I don't?"

She frowned. "The cynicism I hear in your voice. You'd rather I confirmed your jaded view of women, so you can have your proxy marriage and your affairs with a clear conscience. It's easier to blame everything on Chandra and refuse to see that love has triumphed over worse adversity."

He was affected more than he wanted her to see and wondered if she could be right.

Then do something about it, his inner voice insisted. Be the man she already thinks you are. He began to see that he was fighting himself as much as her. He groped for the next stop, for once in his life not at all sure what it should be.

She leaned across the table, her eyes blazing. "I'm not going to change your mind, am I? I can talk all day and night and it won't make any difference. You've made up your mind about love and the last thing you want is an idealistic female confusing the issue with facts. Well, fine. Have it your own way. Love is a con job dreamed up to sell perfume and satin sheets. It doesn't bind two people together for better or worse, or ensure the future of the human race. You'll have your proxy marriage because I believe in honoring my obligations, but I'll make sure you aren't inconvenienced by my feelings for you, since according to your rules, they can't possibly be real. Are you satisfied now?"

Before he could answer, she threw down her napkin, pushed her chair away from the table and flung herself into the pavilion. Moments later he heard her bedroom door rock on its hinges. It was just as well this was a celibate retreat, he thought, or he might have given in and followed her, showing her what real satisfaction meant, for both of them.

He wouldn't because they would have all the time in the world for that after they were married. Buried in her tirade was the answer he had come for. Now all he had to do was make her understand that she had changed his thinking, and what she felt was very, very mutual.

Only then could their future begin.

Chapter Eleven

Caroline wondered if many couples spent their Wedding Eve locked away from each other in separate rooms. Aware of how close she had come to betraying her love for Michel, she had kept to her bedroom for the rest of the evening. It hadn't stopped her from being aware of his every sound as he moved restively around the pavilion. Whenever his footsteps neared her door, her heart gathered speed until it felt as if it might burst from her chest. But he had gone past, closing himself in his own room.

Falling into an exhausted sleep in the early hours, she slept late into the morning. When she emerged, Michel was swimming laps in the pool. Hungrily, she watched his muscular arms and legs churn through the water. He looked as if he was working off some gnawing frustration. At the thought that she could be the reason, a tiny flame of hope flickered to life inside her, but she doused it just as quickly. Last night she had set out to change his cynical view of love without considering how well it served his purpose. She wouldn't make the same mistake again.

By the time she made herself coffee and ate a croissant and some strawberries from a lavish buffet that an unseen servant had set out in the dining room, Michel had disappeared into the changing room alongside the pool. He was whistling, she noticed. Well he might, she thought angrily. He sounded what he was, a man who had everything to gain and nothing to lose.

He returned, wearing a white polo shirt and navy pants, his hair slick with water, and she began to wish they could have the night over again. But she would still feel bound to try to show him that love was worth the fight and the end result would be exactly the same, so what was the point?

He refused her offer of breakfast, informing her that he had already eaten. A car would collect them within the hour, he told her impassively, adding, "Don't be dismayed by the knowing looks we get when we return to the palace. It's another old Carramer tradition to tease a couple returning from their Wedding Eve. If the woman blushes they're suspected of going further than tradition allows."

"Hardly a problem in our case," she said shortly.

"Do you wish it was?"

She looked away, hoping he wouldn't catch her betraying expression. "How could I, when I'm here against my will."

He made a soft tut-tutting sound that brought her head around. His eyes held a devilish gleam. "Still denying reality, Caroline? It wouldn't take much for me to give you a reason to blush when you face the palace staff."

If mental activity counted, she had a reason now, she suspected. "I wouldn't dream of leading you into temptation, Your Highness," she said in a voice that shook only slightly.

She obviously didn't know how sorely he had been tempted to give her that reason to blush last night, Michel thought, refusing to be perturbed. By retiring early she had saved him from further temptation, but he wasn't about to let this go on for much longer. Now he knew how she really felt about him, he had only to resolve one small detail. With luck it would be settled by the time he got back to his office, the reason why he was impatient to be on his way.

"If we had more time, I would show you how far you've already tempted me," he promised, feeling his body tighten as Caroline worked her delicious magic on him. He had never known a woman like her. He wanted to take her to bed here and now, and to perdition with custom, but it wasn't yet time. "Unfortunately, the rest of this discussion will have to wait. I have an important matter to attend to back at the palace."

She tried not to let his impatience upset her although she read it as relief that the Wedding Eve ritual was over. Custom had been satisfied. Now he couldn't wait to get back to his everyday life. And his cynical attitude toward love.

He confirmed her suspicion by taking himself off to his office as soon as they returned to the palace. Although she had expected it, the summary dismissal hurt. At least he didn't know that her heart felt as if it was being squeezed by a steel hand, she thought.

Resolutely, she kept her eyes dry and her head up as she returned to her suite. As his proxy princess, she'd better get used to doing it. The thought that it might be for a long time only made the steel hand close more tightly.

She showered and changed, then changed again, deciding to put on the gold bikini one more time. Cold showers were supposed to work for men. Perhaps a swim could do the same for her. But before she could pull on a cover-up and make her way to the pool, the phone shrilled.

She picked it up. It was Eleanor. "Where have you been? I've been calling since last night," her twin said without preamble.

"With Michel." Caroline hoped that Eleanor wouldn't ask for details.

She was too preoccupied with her own news. "Danny and I had our first big fight yesterday."

Caroline ran a hand through her hair. "What happened? I thought everything was going well."

"It was, until I mentioned in passing that I was considering doing the right thing by you and going to Carramer. Danny hit the roof. He accused me of liking the idea of becoming a princess more than marrying him, then he walked out."

Iced water slid down the length of Caroline's spine. She was terrified that Danny had read Eleanor accurately and her breathing almost stopped. It was Eleanor's right, of course, but every fiber of Caroline's being rejected the idea.

"Are you still there?" her twin asked into the silence.

"I'm here." Could that hoarse voice really be her own? She had to know. "Are you coming to Carramer?"

"Is there a reason why I shouldn't?"

There was only one possible answer. "Not if you're sure it's what you want."

"I thought it's what *you* want," Eleanor said.

Until this moment Caroline hadn't known what she wanted. Now she did. "What I want is to marry Michel if he'll have me."

"But you can't."

The dismay in Eleanor's voice was almost her undoing, but Caroline straightened her shoulders. "Go back to Danny, Eleanor," she said in a world-weary voice. "You love him too much to let a stupid fight split you up. Michel has found out who I am and intends to make me his proxy bride. I intend to let him."

"You would settle for so little?"

"It isn't little if it's the only future worth considering."

"Well, if you're sure? Danny wants to come and talk things over in a couple of hours, but I could be on a plane to Carramer by then."

Her twin's reluctance betrayed her. Eleanor no more wanted to come to Carramer than Caroline wanted to leave. But her willingness to make things right between them touched Caroline more than she could say. "Stay and talk to Danny. Then marry him and be happy," she instructed, not caring if she was falling into the mother role again. It was only for long enough to convince Eleanor that her martyrdom wasn't necessary.

There was a loud sniff down the line. "All right, I will. I do love Danny, you know. You're the greatest sister anyone ever had."

"No, I'm not, I'm in love with Michel, is what I am." Said aloud it had a rightness Caroline could feel to the core of her being.

"Really? That's fantastic. How does he feel about you?"

Caroline took a deep breath. "That's something I'm about to find out."

After saying goodbye to her twin, she didn't wait. Confronting Michel in a gold bikini was probably reckless, but she knew if she took the time to change, her courage might desert her. Wrapping a towel around herself, she set off through the maze of corridors in the general direction of the prince's offices.

If the palace staff found her attire unusual, they didn't show it as they directed her to the wing where Michel was to be found. An assistant guarded his door but swiftly sized up her determination to see the prince then and there, and made it so.

Michel was seated behind a vast antique desk. Evidently his assistant had just finished warning him that she was coming in, because he didn't look in the least surprised. He set the telephone down and steepled his hands in front of him. "You wanted to see me, Caroline?"

At the sight of him, she faltered. It was one thing to tell Eleanor she loved the prince but quite another to tell Michel himself, knowing he didn't want to hear it. "I just had a phone call from my sister," she began.

Instantly he looked concerned. "Is Eleanor all right?"

"She's fine. She offered to come to Carramer and fulfill the betrothal contract."

His expression turned cold and unreadable and she saw him grip the edges of his desk so hard that his knuckles whitened. "And you are here to tell me that you intend to let her?"

"I told her not to come."

He stood up and paced across the room but didn't approach her. "It's just as well," he said, sounding wound tight. "Because the contract is cancelled."

It was the last thing she had expected to hear, and her knees threatened to buckle. Was she too late after all? "I don't understand. How? When?"

He massaged his chin with one hand. "I've had legal experts combing the old statute books. Under an ancient provision, the contract is nullified if either party goes through a second betrothal ceremony with someone else."

She could hardly force the question out, "Have you promised to marry someone else, Michel?"

"No, but Eleanor has, by becoming officially engaged to another man."

Caroline felt hot color rush into her cheeks. She felt like a fool for blundering in unannounced. Now that the contract was void, Michel was under no compulsion to marry her. He probably couldn't get rid of her fast enough. Her declaration of love stalled in her throat and it was probably just as well. This way, she had a chance of retreating with some dignity.

Moving like a robot, she turned toward the door. "In that case, I'd better go and pack."

"Caroline."

He used her name in the tone of a royal command and she froze. "Yes?"

"You didn't know the contract had been cancelled when you insisted on seeing me. Why did you come?"

"It hardly matters now, does it?"

"How do I know unless you tell me what was so urgent you had to come dressed like this? Not that I'm complaining, mind you. But it is a little…unusual."

She had forgotten what she was wearing until she saw his appreciative gaze meander from her bare feet and legs to the towel swathing around her like a sarong. He seemed to have trouble tearing his eyes away from her.

"I apologize for my attire, Your Highness," she said formally. "I wasn't thinking."

His eyes flashed fire. "Then why start now? Why not just tell me what's on your mind."

There was no point denying it any longer. What did dignity matter compared to sharing a heart so full she felt as if it would burst if she didn't share her feelings with him? "I came to tell you that I love you," she admitted. "I know you don't want to hear it now that we don't have to honor the betrothal contract."

"You're wrong," he cut across her, an odd quality in his tone. "I want to hear it now more than ever."

She dragged in air to the limit of her lungs and still felt oxygen starved. What was he saying? "You don't mean to send me away?"

His eyes brightened. "I wouldn't know how."

She lifted her chin, determined to keep at least some semblance of composure, although her heart was beating fast enough to leap out of her chest. The words tumbled from her in a frantic rush. ''Just as well, because I had already decided to stay in Carramer. If I have to, I'll support myself by opening a floral art studio. The idea came to me after seeing all those wonderful tropical flowers in the conservatory.''

He brushed the side of his hand across her cheek. ''I also got a lot of ideas in the conservatory, not one of them to do with flowers.''

''Oh.''

''Are you beginning to get the picture?''

She was almost afraid to, in case she was wrong about this, too. ''It would help if you told me,'' she said in a voice barely above a whisper.

''Then I will, as many times as it takes to make you believe it. I want you to stay, Caroline, and I don't mean in Carramer running some business. I mean here, with me.''

Moving swiftly, he caught her hands and brought them to his mouth, kissing each fingertip in turn with a tenderness that brought tears to her eyes. ''I thought I'd never hear you say it,'' she whispered.

''I thought I would never want to say it. But I want to say it to you over and over again. And when I'm not saying it, I want to show you in every way I possibly can.''

As if to demonstrate he trailed kisses across her bare shoulders until she shuddered with pleasure. Almost afraid of the intensity of her feelings, she looked at him. ''You were so sure you didn't want this to happen.''

What a waste, he thought, wondering how he could have been so shortsighted. He stroked his palm along the waterfall of her hair and was rewarded with a rush of sensual pleasure so intense he wanted to pick her up and carry her over to the chesterfield and make love to her until they could both barely move. Swathed in the towel, her slender body was like a gift-wrapped invitation. It took a great deal to convince himself that he could afford the luxury of waiting, and their time together would be infinitely sweeter for the deprivation. Believing it was another matter.

He made himself concentrate. "As my brother is fond of telling me, love isn't something you command. It commands you, as I found out during our Wedding Eve. After you admitted how you felt..."

Surprise made her gasp. "I did? When?"

He laughed softly. "During your little tirade at the dinner table when you promised not to inconvenience me with your feelings for me. Once I knew you *had* feelings for me, I was forced to examine my own. You were right. I was using one bad experience as an excuse not to risk my heart."

And she had thought she was having no effect on him at all. If she had done nothing else, she had cured him of his cynicism, she thought with a rush of pure love. "And now?" she asked.

"Now I wonder how anyone can live without feeling this way."

She nodded, not trusting her voice.

"All I needed before I could tell you how I felt was the assurance that the contract could be broken." He brushed his lips across her forehead, eliciting a shuddering sigh. "You see, I no longer want a proxy marriage. I want us to have the real thing. Before I could ask you, I wanted to be sure you weren't saying yes out of duty or obligation, but of your own free will this time."

It was so exactly what she needed to hear that she rested her head against his shoulder in pure relief. It brought her towel-clad breasts into contact with the hard wall of his chest, making her aware of the fast beating of his heart. Achingly conscious of how little she was wearing, she tried to step away. She knew she wasn't confusing desire with love, but she was afraid he might be.

The prince would have none of her efforts to retreat. He took positive delight in stroking her shoulders and kissing the line of her neck until her legs turned to jelly. Concepts like dignity and composure were banished from her mind by the only word she could think of right now—surrender. Her heart began to beat ridiculously fast as she threaded her fingers through his hair and pulled his mouth into alignment with hers, putting into her kiss all the love that was his to command from now on.

He gave a low groan as she set about showing him that princes weren't the only ones who knew how to kiss. She had never considered herself very good at it until Michel himself taught her a thing or two. She put his lessons to good use now, brushing her lips across the slight cleft in his upper lip until he gave an explosive sigh and crushed her hard against him, his mouth a heat-seeking missile that homed in on the warm cavern of her mouth.

After what seemed like an eternity, he dragged his mouth away from hers and regarded her through passion-drugged eyes. "We had better make the wedding soon."

Her shining eyes and labored breathing showed that she wasn't about to argue. "Doesn't a royal wedding require months of planning?" she asked, wondering how on earth they were going to be able to endure the waiting.

"This one won't or I may be forced to carry you off to the nearest village and arrange a ceremony in grass skirts presided over by a witch doctor."

Picturing him in native dress was enough to set her pulse raging afresh. "Sounds different," she murmured. "But Carramer doesn't have witch doctors or grass skirts."

"New tradition, by royal decree," he asserted.

She frowned, enjoying the game. "I wonder how I would look in a grass skirt."

He bent and grazed the side of her neck with his teeth, making the blood roar in her ears. "I'd better not start picturing it. You're driving me wild enough wearing a towel. If you were naked from the waist up, I couldn't be answerable for the consequences."

Nor would she. "Then perhaps I'd better get dressed before we cause a scandal. Since you've cancelled the contract, we aren't even betrothed anymore." Odd how she missed it. She hadn't known how much she enjoyed being bound to him until she no longer was.

This other slender thread linking them was too new, too tenuous to really grasp. It came to her that he knew she loved him, and she knew beyond any doubt that he desired her and wanted to marry her, but he still hadn't said he loved her. "Michel?" she asked tentatively.

He heard the uncertainty in her voice and his hold tightened. Resting her head against the padded muscle of his shoulder, she wished she could stay like this forever, melting into his strong arms, holding the world at bay in the timeless wonder of the moment. But it couldn't happen until he told her what she needed to know.

"You haven't said you love me."

He dropped to his knees in front of her. In all his life Michel de Marigny had never kneeled to anyone, but it felt strangely comfortable. With an ease he had never imagined he would feel, he clasped both her hands in his and met her gaze with an intensity he meant her to feel to the depths of her soul. "Caroline Temple, I love you with all my being. Will you marry me?"

All she could manage was a whispered yes before she slid down the length of his body to kneel beside him.

"It won't be easy," he warned her, his throat almost closing with love for her. "A royal life-style has many demands and few rewards."

On her knees, held tightly against him, she gave a quick-silver laugh, picturing the rewards inherent in his promise. She was sure they had nothing to do with titles or posses-sions and everything to do with the love between soul mates. Then she drew back a little. "There is one more thing you should know about me, Michel. It might make a differ-ence."

His eyebrows angled upward. "Only one? I look forward to discovering many facets of you, *ma amouvere*. But if there is something on your mind, by all means tell me."

"I'm not...I mean, I haven't." Tongue-tied suddenly, she wished she had never started this.

But it was already too late. "Are you trying to tell me you have never been with a man?"

She dropped long lashes over brimming eyes. "I'm sorry if I disappoint you."

He threw his head back and roared with laughter then sobered abruptly. "I'm not laughing at you, my beloved, but at your struggle to tell me the one thing any man would give his soul to hear. That you are willing to give to me what you have given to no other man. Disappointed? I am pleased beyond words by such a rare and precious gift. Truly, you are already a princess, my Caroline."

She laughed with him, thrilled to hear him accept as a gift what she had been afraid he might see as a shortcoming. "Then our life together will certainly have its rewards."

Of this he had no doubt. He put into his embrace all the promise of the years ahead. "More than a few, *ma amouvere*."

"Because you're a prince and can order it?" she asked, suddenly filled with a sense of mischief.

He shook his head. "Because it's our destiny."

The very thought of their shared future filled her with a joy almost beyond bearing. There were tears of happiness in her eyes and laughter in her voice as she said, "Who am I to argue with destiny?"

Epilogue

Closing the powder room door behind her, Princess Adrienne de Marigny joined her new sister-in-law, Eleanor Temple, at the mirror. She was still amazed at how like Caroline she was.

Echoing her thoughts, Eleanor said, "I think we should put up a sign that the bride has an identical twin. If anyone else curtsies to me or calls me Your Highness, I may scream. How do you stand it?"

Adrienne laughed. "It's like blue eyes or freckles. When you're born to it, it doesn't seem unusual."

"It's hard to think of my sister as Her Royal Highness, Princess Caroline de Marigny."

"It sounds wonderful to me. She made a beautiful bride."

"She and Michel are a handsome couple, and Prince Lorne is a dreamy best man," Eleanor agreed. "But I thought Prince Lorne's son, Nori, was going to steal the show as the page boy."

Adrienne nodded. "He looks adorable in his little white suit, doesn't he? I'm glad your father made it in time to give the bride away."

It had been touch and go. Apparently, August Temple's boat had run short of fuel somewhere along the Amazon River, forcing him to travel by canoe to the nearest airfield. He had arrived at the Coral Cathedral at Solano with only an hour to spare. Without a bit of royal string-pulling to conjure up formal attire for him, he would have given his daughter away in front of the world's heads of state and a vast array of international media wearing a crumpled safari suit.

"All's well that ends well," Eleanor said on a sigh.

Adrienne finished adjusting her bridesmaid's gown. "We'd better get back to the reception. Caroline will be throwing the bouquet soon."

"I'll probably catch it. My wedding is next." Eleanor turned to Adrienne. "What about you?"

Adrienne felt herself color. "What about me?"

"You're the only one of the royal family still to marry. Perhaps you should try to catch the bouquet."

Adrienne shook her head. "With Lorne and Michel now safely married, I plan to make my escape from royal duties. The last thing I want is a royal wedding."

"Who said anything about royal? There are other men in the world."

"It isn't so simple when you're a princess. The man has to be what my brothers call 'suitable,' even supposing I manage to fall in love."

She was mulling this over as she and Eleanor returned to the banquet hall where the reception was taking place. The baronial hall in the Solano palace was the perfect venue for the lavish reception that had been planned as carefully as a military exercise.

On the arm of Adrienne's gorgeous brother, Michel's wife looked radiant with happiness. Adrienne had never seen Caroline look more beautiful in a white silk Aloys Gada wedding gown, her veil a cascade of antique lace held in place by the diamond-studded coronet that had been Michel's wedding gift to her.

Adrienne joined the rest of the wedding party in the traditional jostle to catch the bride's bouquet. A collective gasp went up as the glorious confection of tropical orchids and baby's breath sailed through the air. Lifting her arm to signal to a friend, Adrienne was startled when the bouquet came toward her. She hadn't meant to catch it, but her hands closed around it instinctively.

Eleanor gave her a playful smile. "See, I told you. Now you'll be the next royal bride."

Adrienne felt her eyes mist as she looked down at the flowers. "To be a bride, one must have a groom," she said, unable to stop a wistful note from creeping into her voice.

Eleanor looked at her curiously. "Maybe I'm seeing romance everywhere, now that Caroline and I have found our soul mates, but there's bound to be a Mister Right, or in your case, a prince, for you, too."

"Maybe I should start kissing frogs."

"Until you do, you never know what they might turn into." Her sister-in-law linked arms with her. "After we see Caroline and Michel off on their honeymoon, we'll have to see if we can find you a pond."

Adrienne smiled. "I suppose the rest is up to me."

* * * * *

She's caught the bridal bouquet.
Will love come Princess Adrienne's way...?

Don't miss THE PRINCESS'S PROPOSAL,
on sale September 2000,
as Valerie Parv's THE CARRAMER CROWN
continues in Silhouette Romance.

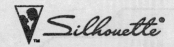

where love comes alive—online...

Visit the *Author's Alcove*

➣ Find the most complete information anywhere on your favorite Silhouette author.

➣ Try your hand in the Writing Round Robin— contribute a chapter to an online book in the making.

Enter the *Reading Room*

➣ Experience an interactive novel—help determine the fate of a story being created now by one of your favorite authors.

➣ Join one of our reading groups and discuss your favorite book.

Drop into *Shop eHarlequin*

➣ Find the latest releases—read an excerpt or write a review for this month's Silhouette top sellers.

➣ Try out our amazing search feature—tell us your favorite theme, setting or time period and we'll find a book that's perfect for you.

All this and more available at

www.eHarlequin.com
on Women.com Networks

USA *Today* Bestselling Author

SHARON
SALA

has won readers' hearts with thrilling tales
of romantic suspense. Now Silhouette Books
is proud to present five passionate stories from
this beloved author.

Available in August 2000:
ALWAYS A LADY
A beauty queen whose dreams have been dashed in a
tragic twist of fate seeks shelter for her wounded spirit
in the arms of a rough-edged cowboy....

Available in September 2000:
GENTLE PERSUASION
A brooding detective risks everything to protect the
woman he once let walk away from him....

Available in October 2000:
SARA'S ANGEL
A woman on the run searches desperately for a reclusive
Native American secret agent—the only man who can save
her from the danger that stalks her!

Available in November 2000:
HONOR'S PROMISE
A struggling waitress discovers she is really a rich heiress—
and must enter a powerful new world of wealth and
privilege on the arm of a handsome stranger....

Available in December 2000:
KING'S RANSOM
A lone woman returns home to the ranch where she was
raised, and discovers danger—as well as the man she once
loved with all her heart....

COMING NEXT MONTH